Flagstick

Bibliography

The Alan Saxon Mysteries
Bullet Hole, 1986
Double Eagle, 1987
Green Murder, 1990
Flagstick, 1991
Bermuda Grass, 2002
Honolulu Playoff, 2004

The Merlin Richards Series
Murder in Perspective, 1997
Saint's Rest, 1999

The Nicholas Bracewell Novels (as Edward Marston)
The Queen's Head, 1988
The Merry Devils, 1989
The Trip to Jerusalem, 1990
The Nine Giants, 1991
The Mad Courtesan, 1992
The Silent Woman, 1994
The Roaring Boy, 1995
The Laughing Hangman, 1996
The Fair Maid of Bohemia, 1997
The Wanton Angel, 1999
The Devil's Apprentice, 2001
The Bawdy Basket, 2002

The Domesday Books (as Edward Marston)
The Wolves of Savernake, 1993
The Ravens of Blackwater, 1994
The Dragons of Archenfield, 1995
The Lions of the North, 1996
The Serpents of Harbledown, 1996
The Stallions of Woodstock, 1998
The Hawks of Delamere, 1998
The Wildcats of Exeter, 1998
The Foxes of Warwick, 1999
The Owls of Gloucester, 1999
The Elephants of Norwich, 2000

The Christopher Redmayne Series (as Edward Marston)
The King's Evil, 1999
The Amorous Nightingale, 2000
The Repentant Rake, 2001

The George Porter Dillman Series (as Conrad Allen)
Murder on the Lusitania, 1999
Murder on the Mauretania, 2000
Murder on the Minnesota, 2002

As Martin Inigo
Stone Dead, 1991
Touch Play, 1991

Flagstick

Keith Miles

Poisoned Pen Press

Poisoned
Pen
Press

Poisoned Pen Press
6962 E. First Ave., Ste. 103
Scottsdale, AZ 85251
www.poisonedpenpress.com
info@poisonedpenpress.com

Printed in the United States of America

*To my many friends in Japan
with thanks for their warm
and lasting hospitality*

Jishin,
kaminari,
kaji,
oyaji.

Earthquakes, thunderbolts,
fires, fathers.
                —Japanese proverb

Chapter One

Only a family funeral could have made me undergo the ordeal of returning home. It was the death of my mother which had driven me decisively away from Leicester for so many long and unforgiving years, and it was the death of her sister that was now drawing me back. Revisiting the scene of so much misery and anguish was a daunting prospect but I felt that I owed it to Aunt Enid. She was one of the few shafts of light in the groping darkness of my childhood, the only adult who ever tried to understand me and to reach me on my own terms. Aunt Enid was the hub of the family, a whirring dynamo of life and laughter, a bubbling extrovert. She was everyone's Happy Person, a true friend at all times, five foot of unassailable optimism. There was something else that made Aunt Enid very special to me. She showed me what my mother might have been if she had not married my father.

Carnoustie hates long journeys as much as I do. She is getting old and cantankerous. What she wants is the leisurely pace of retirement, not a four-hour mad dash in the pouring rain. Within minutes of departure from Kent, she was grumbling noisily and threatening me with all kinds of dire reprisals. Carnoustie is much more than a motor caravan. For most of the year, she is also my base, my command centre and my home. She is a protective travelling companion. Named after the venue of my greatest golfing triumph, she has been a welcome shelter during the all too frequent disasters that have littered my career. Adversity forges bonds. A senile Bedford Aventura knows me better than anyone. The moment I touch her steering wheel, she can sense my mood.

To placate my mutinous partner, I made immediate concessions. We avoided that purpose-built traffic jam known as the M25 and stuck to the major trunk roads. I also spared her the agonies of the M1 on a blustery day when every large vehicle that surged past would have intimidated her with its bulk and buffeted her with its wind displacement. The A6 was slower but far more amenable. Carnoustie still muttered under her bonnet but she nevertheless settled into a steady rhythm. Passing vehicles were the only hazard to her peace of mind. She presented far too big a target for the spray and scum sent up by hissing tyres so she became dirtier by the mile. It put a new note of complaint into her engine whine. Motor caravans have their self-respect.

As we hit open country, the road ahead cleared enough for me to increase speed. Tiring of the radio, I reached into my cassette rack and took out my favourite tape. Chicago were soon reaching into my heart with 'If You Leave Me Now'. The music set off painful memories and I played another tape inside my head.

'Alan?'

'Yes.'

'It's your father.'

'Oh.'

'Enid has died.'

'When?'

'Funeral on Friday.'

Like most of my dealings with my father, the telephone call had been nasty, brutish and short. It had filled me with anger as well as sadness. How had he got my number? I hadn't spoken to him for years and felt myself mercifully free from that barking voice, yet it had penetrated my private domain. The shock had lasted for hours. I got out of Carnoustie and left her doors and windows wide open to get rid of any lingering echo of Thomas

John Saxon. He had tracked me down to my lair and deprived me of all sense of security.

'Enid has died.'

'When?'

'Funeral on Friday.'

The news was not eased by any preparatory remarks or softened by euphemism. He stuck it straight into me like a knife. For a man who had spent his whole life in the police force and who must therefore have often been the bearer of bad tidings, my father was viciously direct. I wondered if he had perfected this technique on the doorsteps of Leicester when he told distraught husbands that their wives had been killed in road accidents, or when he turned agitated women into grieving widows with some equally grim intelligence. Did he inflict maximum pain when he reported the death of children to white-faced parents? No, he must be absolved of that. In all those circumstances, he would be discreet and considerate. He would show due respect. It was only with his son that he could afford to be so abrupt. A life I had once shared with such pleasure was dismissed with a non-committal grunt.

'Enid has died.'

'When?'

'Funeral on Friday.'

My father never answered my questions. If I had asked when the funeral was, he would have told me how she died. It was his way of keeping the initiative. Civil conversation was never his strong point. His forte was the browbeating monologue or the gruff interrogation. A forlorn image of my mother came into my mind.

Chicago were singing 'Where Did The Loving Go?'

I replayed another telephone call.

'Uncle Ted?'

'Who's this?'

'Alan.'

'Who?'

'Alan. Your nephew.'

'Alan!' I could hear the gratitude in his voice bring tears to his eyes. 'God bless you, son! The most dreadful thing has happened, Alan. Your aunt...'

'I heard, Uncle Ted. That's why I rang.'

'Thank you. Thank you.'

'The funeral is on Friday, I'm told.'

'That's right. Eleven-thirty.'

'Which church?'

'St Mark's.'

'I'll be there.'

'Alan!' My announcement threw him into fresh paroxysms of gratitude. 'I can't tell you how much this means to me. I know how busy you are. We thought you might be abroad or something. But if you could come...if you could actually get back to Leicester for the...It would be wonderful. Enid was very fond of you.'

'I'll be there, Uncle Ted. I promise.'

There was a sigh at the other end of the line, then he lapsed into a tale that he had obviously told many times already. It was at once defensive and full of self reproach.

'I was up the Club when it happened, Alan. I mean, I had to be there. I'm the Treasurer this year and we were having a committee meeting. Enid said it was okay for me to go. She was fine when I left the house.' I could hear him wheezing. The effort was rekindling his asthma. 'There was nothing at all wrong with her. Apart from the angina, that is, but we had that under control. She took tablets all the time. Dr Reed said she'd outlive the lot of us. Then...' The wheezing intensified. 'I blame myself, really. I should have been there. By the time I got home...'

Details which would haunt him forever were put on display for yet another member of the family. Uncle Ted was a broken man. He had fed off his wife's vitality for thirty years and gloried in her bustling attentions. All that was now gone. With the death of his wife, his own life-support machine had been switched off. Uncle Ted was posthumous.

'How is the golf?' he asked meekly.

'Not too bad.'

'We don't see your name in the papers so much now.'

'No. Probably not.'

'But you're still Alan Saxon!' he said loyally.

'Yes, Uncle Ted.'

A pause. 'Will you *really* come on Friday, son?'

'Of course.'

'Thank you. That's wonderful. Thank you…'

The contrast with my father could not have been more striking. Uncle Ted was a red-faced, mild-mannered man who inherited the family butcher's shop and spent a lifetime hacking meat into pieces for demanding housewives. He was a hardworking soul with the casual brutality that went with his calling but there was a gentle, easy-going side to him that I liked. His wife gave him a status and confidence that he would not otherwise have had. Her energy fuelled their marriage. As I came off the telephone to him, I could picture his bewilderment and his grief. In its own way, reunion with him at the funeral would be almost as harrowing as meeting my father across another grave. I went over my chat with Uncle Ted once more and searched for comfort in it.

Chicago had moved on to 'You're The Inspiration'.

I coaxed more speed out of Carnoustie and concentrated on the lyrics. They were dedicated to a tiny woman who was now lying in her coffin in a Leicester funeral home.

A stop for petrol broke the tedium of the journey then it was on again towards Kettering. When Market Harborough loomed up ahead, I knew that we were within striking distance of home and my reluctance set in with a vengeance. My foot slackened on the accelerator and a respectable fifty miles an hour became a halting thirty-five. Carnoustie seized the opportunity to throw a tantrum and stall at a traffic island. It took me two minutes to get mobile again.

Leicester is an unlovely city. Ring roads envelop it like concrete winding sheets and sign painters have had a field day. Directions greet you on every side. It is the perfect habitat for my father—an array of imperatives designed to control and subdue. After two early mistakes, I finally took the correct exit from the inner ring road and picked my way through the suburbs. Long, thin streets of terraced houses were narrowed even further by rows of parked cars. Video shops, laundrettes and wine stores abounded. A Chinese restaurant and a snooker hall lent a gaudy colour to the drab scene. Minimarkets bore Asian names above them. The betting shop had its dribble of customers. I was pleased to see that fish and chips had survived into the 1990s.

In the years that I had been away, the city had changed completely and yet remained horribly the same. These mean streets were still redolent with memories of a blighted youth. A father in the police force is a handicap that will plague any child. My schoolmates at the local comprehensive either ignored me or baited me. The few friends I did make suffered along with me. There seemed to be no escape from my father. Having cowed me at home, he pursued me into the classroom to poison my relationships there.

I turned into a wider road and saw lights in the corner shop ahead. Uncle Ted's shop was still open for business. As we cruised past at low speed, I caught a glimpse of a young man wielding a meat cleaver with the murderous precision that my uncle had always shown. It was not difficult to guess what the customers were talking about. My aunt lived and died in the room directly above the shop. Her energy and affability would be sorely missed.

Two more turns brought me within sight of the church and gave me the first jolting hint of my father's presence. St Mark's is one of those neo-Gothic buildings that must have looked suitably impressive in Victorian times when it loomed over the small village whose needs it served. Time had been unkind. Hemmed in by houses and sullied by a century of pollution, it had an air of neglect that was quite devastating. My father had at least cleared away the cars that would otherwise have obscured its blackened frontage even more. A row of No Parking signs created an area of respectability where the hearse could park and the mourners could alight. A uniformed constable was on patrol to enforce the decree of Inspector Tom Saxon.

I parked Carnoustie in a cul-de-sac a hundred yards away and made myself a restorative cup of coffee. There was no point in getting there any earlier than was necessary. It would only expose me even more to gabbling questions and goggle-eyed wonder. Fame has no place at a funeral. I timed my arrival carefully, slipping into the church as the hearse was pulling up outside the gate. Wedged into a pew at the rear, I was spared most of the unwanted attention I feared. My immediate neighbours were customers from the butcher's shop, too weighed down by their own sorrow to take any notice of me, but there were still a few heads that turned to stare balefully at my celebrity.

When the cortége entered, I was shaken and distressed. The smallness of the coffin seemed like an insult to a woman of such large bounty. It was as if a child were being buried, not a sixty-year-old woman with four sons of her own and five grandchildren. The whole family had warmed its hands and its hearts before the roaring fire that was Aunt Enid but all that now remained of her were a few embers in a little pine box. Cremation had preceded burial. Death was at its most reductive.

The service was well under way before I felt able to take stock of my father. He was at the front of the church with the rest of the close family, adding his sonorous bass to the lack-lustre singing of the hymn. The similarities between us were at once apparent. Tall, angular and with close-cropped iron-grey hair, he towered above those around him. We were both easy men to see in a crowd. There the resemblance ended. While he sought the limelight, I preferred the shadows. While he loved authority, I ran away from it. As I looked at the diminutive coffin propped up on trestles, I was reminded of something else about Aunt Enid. It was she who had bought me my first golf set in a children's toy shop and who had taught my infant hands to putt a plastic ball into a metal hole. Those clubs gave me weeks of harmless pleasure until my father destroyed them as a punishment.

'Hello, Alan…'

'Lovely to see you.'

'Where've you been hiding?'

'Great shame, isn't it?'

'Ted will never survive this.'

'She was full of beans last week.'

'Enid would overdo things.'

'How are you, anyway?'

'Saw you on the telly once.'

'Still playing golf, then, are you?'

'Hello, stranger…'

Faces and voices came at me from every direction and I replied with an all-purpose nod. We had moved on to the church hall, a cold and cheerless echo chamber with a few tables set out at one end. Willing ladies served tea, coffee or sherry from trays. Sandwiches and cakes stood waiting. The general gloom was underscored by a sense of relief that the service was over. The vicar mingled with professional ease. I had to work my way through the family.

Uncle Ted was first, pumping my hand by way of thanks and delivering his monologue once again. His sons—my four cousins—greeted me with varying degrees of interest and their wives presented children for inspection. But the real confrontation was with my father. As I saw him bearing down on me, I grabbed a glass of sherry from a tray and downed it in a gulp. A small bonfire started in my stomach.

He began with his usual crashing obviousness.

'You came, then?'

'Yes.'

'Where from?'

'Kent.'

'Train?'

'I drove up.'

'In that clapped-out motor caravan?'

'Carnoustie is my home.'

'That the best you can do?'

He had not mellowed with the years. The same watchful eyes gleamed out of the same hard and embittered face. He exuded the same angry power as he had always done. In deference to his sister-in-law, he had at least worn a suit but it still looked like a policeman's uniform. Even in a private gathering like this, he was patently on duty.

'What about George?' he challenged.

'What about him?'

'Why didn't you come to *his* funeral?'

'I was in Ireland.'

'We found out where. Got a message to the clubhouse.'

'I was playing in a tournament.'

'You could have dropped out.'

'It wasn't possible.'

'Didn't you care about your Uncle George?'

'In some ways.'

'What have you got against my brother?'

'Nothing.'

'So why did you come today?'

'I wanted to.'

'From Kent?'

'Yes.'

'But you couldn't make it from Ireland.'

He was giving me the familiar amalgam of reproach and cross-examination. My father was his own interview room. I glanced around to see if there was a constable at hand to take down every word I said in a ring-topped pad. Both of us knew why I had made no effort to attend the funeral of my Uncle George. He was hewn from the same rock as my father. Each was a born policeman. While Tom Saxon had stayed in the uniform branch all his life, his younger brother had moved into the C.I.D and fought his way into the elite Serious Crimes Squad in the West Midlands Constabulary. At the time of his death, George Saxon had been suspended from duty with many of his colleagues while allegations of police corruption were being investigated.

My father read the disapproval in my face.

'George was an honest copper.'

'I'm sure he was.'

'As clean as a whistle.'

'You're probably right.'

'So don't you dare sneer at him.'

'I'm not sneering.'

'Police work is never easy. It needs a special type.'

He saw my veiled contempt and was about to strike back when a short, bosomy, grey-haired woman in a black coat and black feathered hat waddled up to him. She peered amiably at me through large spectacles then nudged my father with her elbow. Miraculously, he contrived a smile.

'I want you to meet Dorothy.'

'Hello, Alan,' she said, extending a gloved hand. 'I've heard so much about you from your Dad. It was very kind of you to join us today. I know you liked your Aunt Enid.'

'Yes.' I shook her hand. She had a limp grip.

'Your Dad and I have been friends for some time. I've always wanted to meet his famous son. He talks about you a lot when we're together.'

Realisation hit me like a thunderbolt. My father was actually courting this trim little creature. Cold, hard and selfish, he had somehow attracted a warm and caring woman. She had the same gushing timidity that my mother had when I was a baby. I wondered how long it would be before Dorothy had it crushed out of her as well. They made an incongruous pair but something had clearly drawn them closely together. She was beaming up at him and he was raising a roguish eyebrow. It was a side of my father I had never seen before and it embarrassed me.

Dorothy turned back to clutch at my arm.

'Your Dad says that you travel a lot.'

'I have to in my walk of life.'

'All over the world.'

'Just about.'

'Where are you off to next?'

'Japan.'

'Japan!' She repeated, tightening her grasp. 'Oh, I've always wanted to go to Japan, haven't I, Tom? I mean, they're so different from us, the Japanese. So foreign. Have you been there before, Alan?'

'A few times.'

'What's it like?'

'Mind-blowing.'

'I've always wanted to go to Japan.'

'Good police force,' noted my father. 'They rule with a rod of iron. One of the lowest crime rates in the world. I keep up with the statistics.'

Dorothy smiled indulgently. 'He knows so much, Alan. He has a wonderful brain, really.' She mistook my amazement for polite enquiry. 'Yes, you must be wondering how we met. My husband, Glyn, was a policeman, you see. He died some years ago. That's when I met your…that's when Tom and I became friends. We get on so well.'

I would not have minded so much if she had not been such a nice woman. My father was fully entitled to have a woman friend. As many as he liked, in fact. But I was still shocked that my mother had been displaced by someone who gave every evidence of being a carbon copy of her. How do savage men attract such love and devotion? Why hadn't somebody *warned* her? My mind was in turmoil. In the space of a couple of minutes, my whole relationship with my parents was setting off the old torments like a series of fireworks. When would the injuries finally heal? Why did I hate my father so much? Why did I resent the way my mother had given in to him? When would I finally outgrow the damage they had done to me?

Another question now burrowed its way into me.

Was I any better as a father myself?

'Thank you so much for coming, Alan,' cooed Dorothy.

'I must be going.'

'So soon?'

'Only a flying visit, I'm afraid.'

'Your Dad was grateful,' she prompted.

He did not give an inch. 'Ted was pleased,' he said.

'So were you, Tom. Admit it.'

An angel of mercy in a fawn raincoat detached Dorothy from us for a brief consultation. I saw my chance to beat a hasty retreat from an oppressive situation.

'I really must be off.'

'Dorothy wanted to meet you.'

'Oh, yes. She's…very nice.'

'It was her idea to ring you.'

'How did you get my number?'

'From Rosemary.'

It was the final blow. One of the lasting agonies of my doomed marriage was the way that Rosemary, my ex-wife, had got on with my father. In background and outlook, the two of them were worlds apart and yet they had somehow become friends. He was still able to enlist her aid against me and Rosemary was still only too ready to offer it. I mumbled an exit line and tried to move away but Dorothy closed in on me again.

'Have you told him about the book?' she asked.

'What book?' I said.

'*Your* book, of course. The one you wrote.'

'Oh that…'

'We bought a copy.'

I was astounded. 'Why?'

'Tom's your *father*. He's proud of you.' She cued him in. 'Where's the book? Let Alan sign it for you.'

'Doesn't matter,' he said.

'Where is it, Tom?'

'Left it at home.'

'What did you do that for? Alan would've been delighted to sign it for you. It's his autobiography. He ought to put a dedication or something.'

'Next time,' I lied.

'Can't you drop in at the house?' she persisted.

'Next time.'

I moved away to throw a few words of farewell to Uncle Ted then I headed swiftly for the nearest door. Leicester was getting its own back on me. I had paid my respects to Aunt Enid and watched the last bit of joy vanish out of the family. There was nothing there for me now.

I jogged all the way back to the cul-de-sac then drove Carnoustie towards the M1. The most direct route south was needed. As we thundered off down the outside lane, I was glad that I was off to Japan the next day. I wanted to be as far away from home as I possibly could in order to outrun its demons. Somehow I had to break away from its pernicious influence once and for all. But even as Carnoustie tore down the motorway at a reckless speed, I knew in my heart that the prospect of real escape was illusory.

We were *all* going to Japan.

Chapter Two

Heathrow was throbbing with muted resentment as impatient passengers heard about further flight delays. Having left a disgruntled Carnoustie in the long-stay car park, I made my way to the departure lounge and checked in, grateful that my First Class ticket rescued me from an interminable queue alongside the inevitable golf fans who haunt public places (Hello, Alan, I play a bit myself, you know. There's something I've always wanted to ask you) Since I was travelling at someone else's expense, I was able to bask in all the little luxuries that I am not usually able to afford. It was a far cry from the privations of life in a motor caravan. Sparta to Babylon is one great leap.

Thai International is a pleasant and efficient airline with cabin attendants who seem to have been chosen for their effortless geniality. The men wear smart uniforms and the women delight with national dress but both are unfailingly polite and helpful. An orchid presented to every passenger before take-off is a typical gesture. I pinned mine to the back of the seat in front of me so that I could enjoy it to the full before the long flight made it wilt. After twelve hours in the air, I knew that I would end up in the same dry and drooping state as the flower.

My companion was a tall, well-groomed American woman in her forties with an impeccable business suit and an equally impeccable business manner. She was in no way surprised to be sitting next to a long-legged man in a blue track suit, no doubt dismissing it as English eccentricity. We exchanged pleasantries until we were airborne, then she came out in her true colours. The woman was a top international banker who operated between London, Hong Kong and New York, keeping to a schedule that had me gasping in astonishment. A drive to Leicester and back had exhausted me but here was someone who was permanently in orbit and who seemed to thrive on it. She dismissed the notion of jet lag as irrelevant.

It was difficult not to be impressed by her poise and studied charm but—after half an hour—I felt that I had heard all that I wished to about the inner workings of the banking system. To my eternal relief, the conversation soon terminated itself. Pausing only to sip her gin and tonic, she appraised me properly for the first time.

'And what do *you* do?' she said.

'I play golf.'

'Yes, but what's your line of work?'

'That's it.'

'Golf?'

'I'm a pro.'

Incredulity showed. 'You do it for a *living*?'

'Yes.'

'All the time?'

'I like the game.'

She nodded seriously but I had frightened her off. I was as much outside her sphere of experience and interest as she was outside mine. We settled for an uneasy togetherness that was broken only by the occasional remark on a neutral subject. Bankers disturb me at a deep level. It was pleasing to gain a token revenge.

Excellent food, regular glasses of orange juice and a bulky paperback by Len Deighton kept me diverted for hours. When I slipped on my earphones and plugged into one of the music channels, I was touched to find Chicago singing 'Hard Habit To Break'. All my creature comforts were on tap. The first film to be shown was *The Secret Life of Ian Fleming*. It traced his meteoric rise to the highest ranks of the British Secret Service via the bedrooms of a succession of improbable lovelies with foreign accents that had been stuck on like false beards. It was all good, clean, uncomplicated fun in the mock-English mould with the fictional James Bond foreshadowed by the supposedly factual details of the life of his creator.

And yet no real life could have been like this. Nobody inhabits a world of edited highlights seen from clever camera angles. Most of us have long periods of dross between the fleeting glimpses of gold. Even an international banker such as my companion has dull days—I was providing one for her at that moment—yet there is still a lurking compulsion in all of us to pretend that our existence is a source of continuous pleasure and excitement. The film reinforced that myth. In my autobiography, I had challenged it. As a result, I was still suffering at the blood-stained hands of my critics. Truth is not always well-reviewed.

I slept through the second film and awoke in time to eat a light breakfast that was washed down with hot black coffee. Another dip into Len Deighton and we were almost there. As the plane began the slow descent over Thailand, I looked out through the window at huge acreages of flooded land. We were flying over Tropical Monsoon country. People here were accustomed to natural catastrophe. It made me almost ashamed to feel so jangled by my father and by the repercussions in a church hall in Leicester. The Thai population really had something to worry about.

Diplomatic relations with the banker were resumed.

'How long are you staying in Bangkok?' she asked.

'Two days.'

'Playing golf?'

'And seeing friends.'

'Then on to Japan?'

'That's the idea.'

'More golf?'

'I'm afraid so.'

We taxied to a halt then I took my leave of her. The plane was flying on to Hong Kong where she would tell her astonished colleagues about the strange being she had met in transit. Alan Saxon would enliven the discussion in her air-conditioned boardroom. One way or another, my bizarre choice of profession has a habit of causing flutters in banking circles. This time, at least, no overdraft was involved.

Don Muang Airport is one of those huge, gleaming, ultramodern buildings entirely lacking in character. Vast sums of money have been lavished upon it but the net result was a kind of ostentatious invisibility. It made me want to get on through customs and out. With my reclaimed suitcase and golf bag loaded onto a trolley, I made my way across the covered bridge towards the Airport Hotel. Warm air hit me at once and clung to me like a thick blanket. My track suit turned the two-minute stroll across the bridge into a walk through a furnace. I found myself longing for the chilly English autumn that I had left behind.

At the entrance to the hotel, porters took charge of my luggage and I was able to glide down to Reception on the escalator and check in. A soundless lift then took us up to the third floor and opened to reveal wide, thickly carpeted corridors going off in different directions. My youthful porter located my room, showed me in, parked my luggage, gave me a prize-winning grin when I tipped him and backed out. More luxury surrounded me. My bedroom was large and well-appointed with anything and everything that the needy traveller might want. The bed was so big and welcoming that I could have parked Carnoustie on one side and still had plenty of room for myself.

Though it was only morning in Bangkok, it was well past midnight on my own biological clock. I had a quick bath to relax me, closed the curtains to shut out the bright sunlight then slipped in between the sheets. The next four hours were spent in blissful slumber.

An insistent ringing sound brought me back to reality. I reached out for the bedside telephone and tried to clear my head as I put the receiver to my ear. My voice was a sleepy whisper.

'Yes?'

'Is that you, Alan?'

'Speaking…'

'Oh dear. I have woken you up.'

'No, no,' I said through a yawn. 'Who is this?'

'Sam Limsong.'

'Nice to hear from you.'

'Not when you are fast asleep. Jet lag?'

'Just having a nap.'

'Then I will not keep you,' he said. 'I just rang to fix a time for tomorrow. We are playing at The Rose Garden.'

'Great!' Another yawn. 'Sorry, Sam.'

'I'll pick you up early at your hotel.'

'How early is early?'

'Six o'clock.'

'I'll be waiting.'

'See you tomorrow, Alan. And by the way…'

'Yes?'

'Welcome to Bangkok.'

Sam Limsong's chirpy voice vanished just as I was coming fully awake. We had met a few times at tournaments over the years but it was in a Skins Game in Australia that we had got to know each other slightly better. Sam was not only Thailand's leading golfer, he had also established himself as the outstanding talent in the Far East by supplanting Yokuri Tanizaki. He was young, committed and very ambitious. Sam had promised to play a round with me next time we were both in Bangkok together. That time had come.

I dressed and went downstairs for a late lunch in the Zeppelin Coffee Shop, then it was off downtown in the hotel shuttle bus. Road travel in Bangkok is not for the faint-hearted. The main thoroughfares have the kind of permanent traffic jams that make the M25 look almost deserted. Law-abiding drivers would stay motionless forever. You have to bully, create gaps, dart forward, change lanes and use your horn incessantly. Ears still buzzing and nerves frayed, I was deposited near a large department store with the other passengers. Shopping is something that I normally avoid at all costs but today was different. Bangkok both guaranteed me an anonymity that I never enjoy in my own country and it offered me a range of options that was irresistible. It was a refreshing change of habit and habitat for me.

After a lengthy trawl of the store and the galleries of shops all around it, I ventured out into the early evening crush and let the wave of bodies carry me for a few blocks until we came to a set of traffic lights. I crossed the road in front of a line of assorted vehicles—revving away as if they were on the starting-grid in some Grand Prix—and went into the real paradise for the bargain-hunter. The street market had everything. A continuous line of rickety tables displayed the most amazing variety of wares. Shops, stalls and arcades multiplied the choice and widened the opportunity for mild chaos. Haggling was of the essence. The final price of any item was a compromise between the buyer's persistence and the vendor's tenacity.

It was noisy, sweaty, smelly and enormous fun. Elbowing my way through the crowd, I ransacked tables and explored shops until my arms were full of presents. Only when I paused for breath did I realise what I was doing. Everything I had was for my daughter. Lynette was the one person in my life who brought me untrammelled joy. A fifth-former in an expensive public school was my only real family. I had to tell her that somehow. My trip to Leicester made me want to shower her with presents and—hopefully—shore up her love with my impulsive generosity. Lynette did not need any of the items for which I had haggled so assiduously but I needed to sent them nevertheless. Guilt sent me out on that shopping spree.

Traffic had thickened by the time I was picked up by the hotel bus and the return journey was even more hair-raising. Our driver corkscrewed his way through the serried ranks of vehicles as if in the grip of some death wish, but he somehow got us all back safely to the hotel. It was still only eight o'clock but an early night was mandatory. After a light supper in the Coffee Shop—now staffed by even more willing waitresses with a wonderful Thai smile—I took my armful of purchases off upstairs to view them at leisure. I was tired but quietly reassured. My trip downtown had put a layer of insulation between me and my father. Concentrating on Lynette had helped events in Leicester to recede in the memory. I went into my room in a mood of cautious hope.

It was shattered at once. As soon as I switched on the lights, I sensed the intrusion. Someone had been into my room in my absence. It was not just the hotel maid who had turned down my bed. It was a visitor with no legitimate reason to be there. I tossed the presents on the bed and conducted a quick search of the room to see if anything had been taken or moved. All seemed perfectly in order but the faint air of menace still hovered. A malign presence had been there. I double-locked the door but it brought me no comfort at all.

My precautions were too late.

◇◇◇

Sam Limsong arrived punctually next morning in a shining Toyota Estate. He was wearing shirt, slacks and the straw trilby that had become so well-known on the golf courses of the world. Tall and cadaverous, he had the easy arrogance of the consistent winner but it was tempered by an odd humility in the company of a guest from Europe. The son of a wealthy industrialist, Sam was a member of the elite, a rich man in a poor country, an international celebrity among the faceless millions. I loaded my golf bag into the car then got into the passenger seat beside him.

'How's the hotel?' he said.

'Fine, fine.'

'Sorry to get you up at dawn.'

'No trouble.'

'I hope you managed to get enough sleep.'

'I did, I did.'

But it was a lie. The sense of invasion had disturbed me all night and I had only drifted off for a few merciful hours. I considered a protest to the management but I had no evidence to offer beyond my instinct. The anxieties of an English tourist were hardly reason enough in themselves to alert the security staff. I would simply have to be very careful and very watchful.

Sam Limsong drove due west along a dual carriageway. He glanced across to give me a broad grin.

'Good to see you again, Alan.'

'Thanks.'

'I keep track of you when I can.'

'Not much to keep track of this season,' I admitted. 'It's been one of those years, Sam. I've played good golf but the others have always played better. The Jersey Open was the only time I even scraped into the top ten.'

'Consistency is always a problem.'

'Not for me. I've been consistently out of luck and consistently short of prize money.' We shared a laugh. 'But that's the way it goes. I'll be back one day.'

'You always come through in the end.'

'It's the Saxon trademark.'

Sam Limsong had had a promising if unspectacular season so far on the U.S.P.G.A Tour with enough winnings to get him comfortably into the top twenty on the Money List. The latest Sony World Ranking had him in eleventh position, well ahead of any other Far Eastern player. Yokuri Tanizaki, the Japanese master, had fallen away to the spot. Back trouble had forced my host off the circuit for three weeks and given him the opportunity to fly home to Thailand. Ample compensation awaited him.

'I am getting married next month,' he said.

'Congratulations!'

'Somjai is very beautiful.'

'Like all the rest of the female population.'

'Thai girls are special,' he agreed, then his grin faded. 'It is a pity that Europeans only know about the ones who work in the nightclubs and massage parlours. They give the rest of the girls a bad name.' His chin jutted out proudly. 'Thai woman are the loveliest in all Asia. And my Somjai is the loveliest of the lot.'

'Is she interested in golf?'

'She will be.'

'How did you meet her?'

'In hospital.'

'Oh?'

'Somjai is a physiotherapist.' He threw me a smirk. 'If I am going to have back trouble, I may as well enjoy it. She knows how to put me right.'

'Good luck to both of you!'

'Thanks.'

'Marriage has a lot going for it.'

I tried to sound positive on a subject that would always be weighed down with negatives for me. When I'd married Rosemary, I had the same hopes and ambitions and unshakeable certainties as Sam Limsong. If I was honest, I also had the same fantasies about curative massage at the hands of my wife. Golf changed all that. It opened a gap between us that widened imperceptibly into a chasm. Divorce was inevitable. I would not wish that experience on anybody.

He tuned in to my wavelength at once.

'I'm sorry that it did not work out for you, Alan.'

'Luck of the draw.'

'There is more to it than that, I think.'

'Maybe.'

'Do you still see Rosemary?'

'How do you know her name?'

'I read your book.'

'Ah.'

'I bought a copy in New York.'

He was the second unexpected reader of my memoirs but a far more acceptable one than my father. I was flattered by his interest. *Shadows on the Grass* was not the usual recital of successes by a golfing superstar. My mistake was to begin too young and peak too early. At the time when Alan Saxon won the British Open at Carnoustie all those years ago, it was not the passport to instant wealth that it is now. I had enormous kudos and a lot of public exposure but they only worked against me. Built up so high, I had a fearsome way to fall and it was painful when

I landed. *Shadows on the Grass* was abrasively honest about the pitfalls of professional golf. Each of us has only a limited share of the sun.

'There was very little about your family,' said Sam.

'That was deliberate.'

'I'd like to have known more about your parents.'

'They weren't relevant.'

'My father has been behind me all the way.'

'So has mine—that's why I keep on the move.'

My parents had been given only a brief mention in the Foreword. It was more difficult to erase Rosemary because my publisher had insisted on a wedding photo as well as some snaps of Lynette. They made me wince whenever I opened the book, but I had come to acknowledge them as vital pictorial aspects of my past. Besides, my title did not only refer to setbacks on a never-ending series of golf courses. There was the personal side to it. My father and my wife both cast very long shadows indeed.

'Your book stirred a few people up,' he noted.

'That was the idea.'

'I liked it.'

'Then you're in the minority, Sam.'

'The reviews I saw were not too bad.'

'They were dreadful,' I said with a laugh. 'The first batch were so poisonous that my publisher refused to send them to me. When I asked him what they were like, he called them "a mixed bag". That means they were pure cyanide.'

'You did attack a lot of people.'

'Only because they attacked me first.'

'What have you got against golf writers?'

'They sit in judgement.'

We turned to brighter topics and the journey seemed to be over in a matter of minutes instead of the best part of an hour. The Rose Garden is a relatively new golf course in an idyllic setting in Sam Phran District. It is the sort of place to which I would love to retire one day, a green and tranquil haven from the workaday world. Though it has a dreamland quality about it, The Rose Garden is no place for lotus eaters. Extending to a full 7,085 yards, the course features gentle mounding, mature trees and strategic water that make it a worthy test from the back tees. In true horticultural vein, each hole is devoted to a particular species of flower, grown in profusion alongside the tee to add even further colour and fragrance.

When we had parked the Toyota and changed in the new clubhouse, we strolled out to be greeted by a veritable army of female caddies. Over four hundred are employed at the course and the two assigned to us by the rota were totally charming. As I soon discovered, there was much more to them than a smart uniform and a bright red straw hat. They were fully inducted into the mysteries of club selection, choice of shot and line of putt. They were also a marvellous giggling audience for any comical remarks that we made along the way. A female caddie in Australia had once landed me neck-deep in all kinds of trouble. My ever-courteous guide at The Rose Garden turned a pleasure into a rare experience.

Sam Limsong was a competitor. Even a round of golf with a friend brought out the fighting spirit in him and he was determined to yield nothing. At the same time, he was testing out his back after rest and treatment, making sure that he was fit enough to return to the rigours of the U.S.P.G.A Tour. Whatever the magic fingers of his fiancée had done to him, it had patently worked. He was strong, supple and hitting the ball as hard as ever. I matched him for length from the tee but my driving was more wayward. He was three strokes ahead at the turn where we were met by a waiter bearing iced tea on a silver tray. The Rose Garden grew rosier all the time. As we marched down each well-manicured Bermuda fairway, I marvelled afresh that the course had been laid out on what was once a flat rice paddy. It was a remarkable act of reclamation.

Another was needed if I was to overhaul my playing partner but the game proved beyond reclaim. His superior knowledge of the course and his sharper edge kept him in front all the way and, though I narrowed the gap slightly with a trio of birdies on the back nine, I blew my chances completely by finding water from the tee on the 18th hole. Guided by the splash, a small, olive-skinned 'klong' boy dived in at once to retrieve it with the excited urgency of a water spaniel. As he surfaced again, he held up my ball in triumph and we applauded. When he brought it back to me, he would only take a few baht from me as a tip, the equivalent of about 5 pence. It seemed small recompense for his heroics and I tried to offer him the ball itself as a souvenir, but he would not hear of it.

The early start had been essential. When we completed our round, the heat was becoming quite fierce and the prospect of a cooling beer in the clubhouse was very appealing. Sam Limsong handed his putter to his caddie and raised his hat politely to me.

'Thank you, Alan.'

'Thanks for inviting me.'

'My pleasure. One question, my friend.'

'Fire away.'

'Why were you talking to yourself on the greens?'

'Oh that…'

'Yes,' he said. 'Every time you stood over a putt, you seemed to be saying something. Was it a prayer?'

I laughed. 'If it was, it didn't bloody well work, did it? No, Sam, I was just practising, that's all.'

'Practising what?'

'Well, my main reason for going to Tokyo is to make this instructional video. They're going to fit a microphone to me so that they can hear my innermost thoughts each time I have to assess a shot. Speak-as-you-play. I thought I'd try it out here but it was quite distracting.'

'Some golfers talk the ball into the hole.'

'I'm the strong, silent type.'

He grinned. 'Who are you making the video for?'

'One of the big multi-nationals.'

'What's the name?'

'Ogino.'

His face hardened. 'Who are you dealing with?'

'Why?'

'Shohei Ogino himself, I bet.'

'That name does ring a bell.'

'He loves golf. Far too much.'

'I'm not with you.'

'Be careful, Alan. That's all I say.'

'Do you know this man?'

'Oh yes,' he said ruefully. 'I know Shohei Ogino.'

'What's wrong with him?'

There was a measured pause before the grin came out beneath the straw trilby once more. He waved a dismissive hand.

'Nothing. You will have a good time in Japan. They pay very well.' He led me towards the clubhouse. 'This heat is even getting to me. We both need a cool shower and a drink.'

'Tell me about this Shohei Ogino…'

But he ignored the question and talked about his forthcoming marriage instead. His evasiveness only served to deepen my unease. If there was some reason to beware of my Japanese host, I wanted to know what it was but Sam Limsong had clearly said his last word on the subject. The seeds of doubt took immediate root. When we reached the clubhouse, I turned back to take a last fond look at a course which blended scenic beauty with a subtle examination of my skills. The Rose Garden was bathed in a sunlight that brought out its deepest hues but Sam's warning had somehow distorted my view of it. I saw only one thing.

Shadows on the grass.

◇◇◇

Bangkok is positively bristling with new experiences for the average British visitor and many cannot wait to explore this fabled nightlife. Commercial sex has never had the slightest appeal for me, not least because of the fact that I have a daughter of my own and a deep if largely undefined concern for her moral welfare. Fatherhood *can* sometimes humanise. The novel experience which the city bestowed on me occurred in the departure lounge just before midnight. As the two hundred and more passengers waited for the signal to board the aircraft, I became aware that I was the only European among them. Japanese holidaymakers made up the bulk of the passenger list with a sprinkling of Thai and other Asian faces in amongst them. I was conspicuous by my presence.

It was strangely unthreatening. On the whole, Japanese are a polite and unassertive people. They may not trust the foreigner but they know how to conceal their prejudice. I was surrounded by nods and smiles and an air of acceptance. It would not have been the same in my own country. A lone Japanese among a comparable number of British passengers would not have been accorded the same tacit welcome. Jokes about slanting eyes and wily Orientals would have been obligatory. Imported Japanese cars would have raised even more sniggers. We would be lost without the Funny Foreigner.

The feeling of being among friends was increased by the smiles of the ever-attentive cabin attendants. Individual orchids again lent their fragile beauty. Tokyo was just under six hours away. My travelling companion this time was a middle-aged businessman with a twinkle in his eye that suggested he half recognised me, but the language barrier saved me any enquiry. As the plane soared into the night sky, I was able to relax and reflect. After the snack was served, I drifted gently asleep.

We were beginning the descent over Japan when I finally came awake and I thought for one moment that I was now in a different aircraft. Gone was that sense of ease and general affability. The atmosphere was taut and even the man beside me seemed to exude a distant hostility. It was the feeling I had had in my room at the Airport Hotel, that instinct for survival that alerts you to an unspecified danger without giving you any clear indication of what it is. I was not among friends, after all. I was being watched. One potential enemy had transformed a restful flight into a source of quiet fear.

I stood up on impulse and looked around but the person concerned was not available for comment. A lurch up and down the aisle brought me no closer to an identification. Having basked in a communal welcome, I now felt completely isolated from everyone aboard. It was inexplicable. When I returned to my seat for the plane to land, however, I knew one thing for certain. I was arriving in Tokyo with more than a suitcase and a set of golf clubs.

I was carrying excess baggage.

Chapter Three

The uniformed chauffeur was waiting for me in the Arrivals Lounge. Unlike most of the drivers, he did not need to hold up the name of his passenger on a placard. One glance told him who I was and he took my trolley from me with masterful ease. He belonged to the Staccato School of English.

'Mr Saxon. I take. This way.'

'Oh, right.'

'Welcome. Tokyo.'

'Thanks.'

'I drive. Nice day.'

'Good.'

'We go.'

That seemed to exhaust his command of the language because he lapsed into a contented silence. Minutes later, I was sitting in the rear of a gleaming Nissan as it pulled away with a controlled surge of power. I glanced nervously over my shoulder and peered through the window but nobody was following us. Whatever danger had lurked on the plane itself had been shaken off. I settled back in my seat for what I knew would be a prolonged journey. Narita Airport is some forty miles east of the city and the expressway that leads away from it gives promises that it does not finally honour. Though you can zoom along in the outside lane for a large part of the way, the traffic slows as soon as you approach the environs of Tokyo. By the time you have picked your way through the outer suburbs, you are down to a crawl. Speed limits take on a mocking note. They are less official commands than impossible targets. Nobody has ever achieved them during the rush hour.

Having been to Japan a number of times, I was familiar with its accelerating golf craze. When buildings began to loom up beside the expressway, therefore, I was not surprised to see a new three-tier golf range for the aspiring Alan Saxons of suburban Tokyo. Equipped with high catch nets, the building gave its customers the dubious privilege of hitting golf balls some thirty yards or so at a rudimentary target on a square of white material that flapped in the wind. Men and women flock to such places to indulge in this weird pastime which always strikes me as the golfing version of simulated sex—the best bit is always missing.

Bigger ranges, with individual cubicles for their eager clientele, do allow you to drive off into catch netting a few hundred yards away, but even this should only be a means to an end, a place for practice and fine-tuning. Unhappily, for most of the country's golfers—and there are over sixteen million of them—it's an end in itself. They get through an entire playing career without ever setting foot on a real golf course. It's rather like learning to swim without actually getting in the water or riding a horse that never leaves its stable.

I was glad when my chauffeur at last found an exit from the elevated dual carriageway on which we had been doing our impersonation of a giant snail. We actually reached fifteen miles an hour as we plunged down into the city itself. Bright sunshine was gilding the skyscrapers but there was no concession to the beauty of the morning by the thousands of pedestrians who were hurrying to their offices. Wearing smart suits and carrying smart briefcases, the business executives of the nation's capital walked briskly over clean pavements with their polished shoes. The sense of order and purpose was quite overwhelming. None of the lurching anarchy or the dawdling indecision you would find on the streets of London. Here are citizens who know exactly where they have to go and what they have to do when they get there.

We reached the centre of Tokyo and followed the one-way system until it delivered us outside the towering bulk of the Imperial Hotel, a breathtaking monument to all that is most daunting about modern architecture. In a frugally minded city where space is used to the optimum, the hotel is an example of ruinous extravagance. The lounge could double as an aircraft hangar and the eleven hundred or more rooms all have generous proportions. As I sailed in through the entrance, I felt as if I was committing an act of adultery for which Carnoustie would never forgive me.

I checked in at the counter hen turned to find an immaculate porter waiting for me with my luggage. Before I could let him conduct me upstairs, however, I was hailed by a voice that has rasped its way through the hotels of the world.

'Saxon!'

Clive Phelps was bounding towards me with outstretched arms. His face looked more ravaged than ever but the curly hair and the bushy moustache still had their old luxuriance. On anybody else, the golf shirt and the cream trousers would have looked casually smart but Clive made them a focal part of his crumpled neglect. The half-smoked cheroot did not leave his lips as he gave me a welcoming embrace.

'How *are* you, matey?'

'Stop trying to set me on fire and I'll tell you.'

'Sorry.' He took the cheroot from his mouth and stepped back. 'Great to see you, old son.' An expansive arm waved. 'Hey, isn't this place fantastic?'

'A bit too cramped for my liking.'

'Wait till you see your room. Palatial.'

'Sounds good to me.'

'It is. So you remember who got it for you, okay? If Uncle Clive hadn't waved his magic wand, you'd be sitting at home in that depressing box on wheels, listening to the rain drumming down on the roof. Motor caravans are so naff.'

'Only to the uninitiated.'

'It's time you saw how human beings lived.'

'I'd prefer to spend my time with you.'

'Turd!'

'You always were very free with compliments.'

'Ungrateful bastard!'

It was time to guide him towards the lift. My track suit and his ebullience were combining to provoke comment in the sober-suited surroundings. With my porter in tow, we went up to the fourth floor and let ourselves into my room. It was indeed palatial. As soon as we were left alone, Clive flopped into the armchair and snatched up the telephone with a lordly air. After one last pull on the cheroot, he stubbed it out in the ashtray on the onyx table.

'Ready for brekky?'

'I could be tempted.'

'How hungry are you?'

'Continental breakfast will be fine.'

'Croissants or rolls?'

'Rolls.'

'I always have croissants,' he said with a nostalgic beam. 'Sentimental reasons. They remind me of someone I met at the inaugural tournament at the Golden Haze Golf Club.'

'I remember her only too well, Clive.'

'Little darling from Rosario. In Argentina.'

'And you did your bit for international friendship.'

'She had this trick with a warm croissant…'

'You've told me many times. It was enough to put me off the things for life. Now order my roll and ask for orange juice as well, please.'

'You'll get it. Freshly squeezed.'

Clive dialled for Room Service and gave instructions, then he lolled in the chair to assess me properly. His moustache rippled above a wicked leer.

'How was Bangkok?'

'Enormous fun. I went on a shopping spree.'

'That's what *I* always do. No city in the world gives you the same feeling of money well-spent. If you know where to go, you can have the time of your little life. There's this one bar I should have recommended to you.'

'Thanks for sparing me.'

'It would've been an education for you, Saxon,' he said. 'Opened your eyes to the full potentialities of the female body. First time I went there...'

'The banana story. I've heard it.'

'Didn't it turn you on?'

'Frankly, no. It just put bananas on the proscribed list along with croissants. The horrors of your sex life have a beneficial effect on my diet.'

'Where's your sense of adventure?'

'I save it for the golf course.'

He gave a raucous laugh and lit another cheroot while I unpacked my case and put my things away. Clive Phelps is a cherished friend. As a golf writer, he's one of the best in the business with a deep knowledge of the game culled from years of unflagging service to it. With hard work and total commitment, he could have become an outstanding player but he is too fond of directing his unflagging service to the bars and bedrooms of the circuit. A promising career was wilfully dissipated in the arms of long-forgotten lovers but he can still write like an angel and he has remained touchingly loyal to Alan Saxon.

He blew a smoke-ring then underlined the fact.

'I'm the only one you've got left, old son.'

'The only what?'

'Friend.'

'That's nothing new.'

'You certainly know how to alienate my colleagues,' he said. 'Mention your name in the Press Tent and it's like a bomb alert. Everyone goes running.'

'They've dropped a few bombs on me before now.'

'Doesn't mean you have to nuke the whole profession.'

'I wrote what I felt, Clive.'

'That was your first big mistake.'

'Eh?'

'You should have got one of us to ghost it,' he argued. 'That way, we could have toned down some of the bile and given your tarnished image a much-needed lick of paint. Golf writers are very proprietory. Trespassers are prosecuted.'

'Then hanged, drawn and quartered in purple prose.'

'Don't come to me for sympathy. Your book had more than its share of executions. *Shadows in the Grass* indeed! It should have been called *Blood in the Bunker.*'

'You came out of it very well, Clive.'

'Yes!' he moaned. 'And where does that leave me with my fellow-scribes? As the odd man out. It would've been far better for me if I'd been torn to shreds along with the rest. At least I wouldn't have had to field so much flak on your behalf. Guilt by association is no picnic.'

'I'm entitled to my opinion.'

'Balls! You're a professional golfer. You only *play* the fucking game. We *define* it.'

We sparred on until the waiter arrived with a trolley. Clive fell on his first croissant with open relish. It soon struck up a close relationship with his moustache. Having hung up the last of my shirts, I sat opposite him and sipped my orange juice. It was Clive Phelps who had effectively brought me to Japan because he had negotiated the deal to produce an instructional golf video. I was to pass on my words of wisdom: he was to provide the commentary. It was a joint venture which had three main attractions for me. As well as taking me once more to a country that I happen to like—despite, and perhaps because of it, its idiosyncrasies—the trip rescued me from a dying fall at the end of a very disappointing season on the European Tour. The financial inducement was also strong. It would be nice to have one Christmas without a broadside from my bank manager.

When Clive stopped chewing his rich memories of a girl from Argentina, I took the opportunity to probe for details.

'Tell me about our sponsors.'

'Ogino Electrical? One of Japan's industrial giants.'

'What do they make?'

'What do you think they make—cream doughnuts!'

'Televisions, transistor radios, personal stereos?'

'And all the rest,' he said. 'Video machines, video cameras, hi-fi systems, cassette players, electric shavers and just about every domestic appliance from vacuum cleaners to vibrators. Then there's the whole telecommunication side of it. The Ogino empire is mind-boggling.'

'What sort of a man is Shohei Ogino?'

'Slightly richer than you and me. Put it this way, old fruit. Shohei Ogino is one of the supermen behind the new super-power. If fancy ever seized him, he could afford to put the Imperial Hotel on wheels and drive it around like Carnoustie. That answer your question?'

'No. I'm talking about his personality.'

'Japanese businessmen don't *have* personalities.'

'Is he someone we can trust?'

'We've got this far, haven't we?'

'Be serious, Clive.'

'A contract is a contract.'

'Have you actually met this character?'

'Shohei Ogino? Yes—once.'

'Well?'

'It was at a tournament in Osaka. His company sponsored the event so he presented the cheque to the winner. I got to interview him along with a couple of other journalists.'

'How did he come over?'

'Courteous, shrewd, mad about golf.'

'Any skeletons?'

'Yes. He's hooked on drugs, keeps fifteen mistresses and buggers the houseboy twice a week. Oh, yes, and he lies about his age so that he can get a Senior Citizen Bus Pass.' He slapped his leg in irritation. 'What is this, Saxon? The man is giving you an expenses-paid fortnight in his country and you start digging for dirt.'

'It was just something that Sam Limsong said.'

'Don't listen to gossip.'

'It was more than that.'

'Then let's hear it.' He did and he was very sceptical. 'Forget it. Sounds like a case of sour grapes.'

'Sam *knows* Shohei Ogino.'

'So do millions of other people. For a man who can rub shoulders with a garden dwarf, Ogino keeps a very high profile. Sam is bound to have met him on the circuit here and raised that bloody straw trilby at him.'

'It made me wonder, that's all.'

'Listen, you put the Thai wonder out of your mind. If you ask me, it's a simple case of jealousy. Sam Limsong likes to be cock of the walk. The thought of real competition wipes that look-at-me grin off his face.'

'Competition?'

'From the rising Japanese star.'

'Which one?'

'Fumio Ogino.'

'Is he any relation to…?'

'Of course,' said Clive. 'Shohei's youngest son.'

I took the news on board. 'How good is he?'

'You'll be able to judge for yourself this afternoon.'

'What do you mean?'

'We're meeting them both at the course. Along with the rest of the entourage, no doubt. Largely a publicity stunt so you'll be expected to pose for lots of photos.'

'Do I need to bring my bikini?'

'You simply need to be on good form.'

'Why?'

'Because they'll want you to show off a bit. Hit a few screamers. Play some of your favourite shots. Demonstrate your delicate touch with the putter.' He jabbed a warning finger at me. 'Shohei Ogina wishes to see that he's made a sound investment in you. Prove it.'

'I can't just dazzle to order.'

'Force yourself. And remember that you're British.'

'Why?'

'You'll see when we get there. It'll be you and me in the middle of hundreds of wealthy Japs. We've got to remind them that Britain can still beat them at one thing.'

'What's that?'

'Golf, you idiot! We're not just here to make a video and pass on our expertise to the waiting millions. We have to do something else as well.'

'Do we?'

'Yes,' he said. 'Fly the flag.'

◇◇◇

Wada International Country Club was just over thirty miles to the west of Tokyo. Our chauffeur-driven limousine took almost an hour to get there via the expressway. A long bath, a short nap and a quick snack had freshened me after my flight and I felt ready to face the reception committee that awaited us. Clive used the journey to brief me about my schedule over the next few days and to get my outline approval on his commentary script. He had mapped out the whole video on a tee-to-green basis with particular attention given to eliminating common faults. The points at which I would speak directly to camera were mercifully few in number but there were sequences—in heavy rough, in a bunker, sinking a putt—when I was required to talk my way through a shot as I played it. I suspected that much of our rehearsal time would be taken up by this latter area. Self-consciousness is a limiting factor.

'Will it take two whole weeks?' I asked.

'Probably not but it's best to be on the safe side. We never know what the weather's going to do. This may be the Land of the Rising Sun but it can have a lot of falling rain at this time of year.'

'What about the camera crew?'

'They'll be highly professional, I'm sure. I spoke to the director yesterday and she sounded very clued up.'

'*She?*'

'Chiyo Takumi.'

'I thought Japan was still resolutely anti-feminist.'

'Times are changing,' he said. 'Chiyo graduated at some American film school. She speaks pretty good English if you don't mind a faint whiff of Texas drawl.'

'Does she know anything about golf?'

'She had a handicap of nine.'

I was pleasantly surprised. 'Where did Ogino find her?'

'He wanted the best. Chiyo Takumi fits the bill. So do Alan Saxon and Clive Phelps. This is top-quality stuff.'

'So what's the catch?'

'You have to do a spot of tap dancing.'

'Oh, no!'

'It was in the small print of the contract.'

'I hate corporate golf.'

'The odd few rounds with the odd few businessmen,' he said. 'That's all they ask. Shohei Ogino wants to display his trophy to his friends. It's not every day the local captains of industry get the chance to play golf with a former Open Champion. Give them a treat.'

'I'm not in a treat-giving mood.'

'And less of the artistic temperament, please.'

'Why wasn't I told in advance?'

'Because I knew you'd raise unreasonable objections.'

'Is it unreasonable to want some control over where and with whom I play a round of golf?' I urged. 'I'm a sensitive soul, Clive. I have feelings. I don't like being rented out to the visiting executives like a set of clubs.'

'See it as a chance to sharpen up your own game.'

'Plodding around at their pace? I need to be put under pressure before I start to function properly. You know that only too well.'

'When in Rome, do as the Romans do.'

'When in Japan, do what Shohei Ogino commands.'

'In essence, yes,' he admitted. 'He who pays the piper.'

'Can we skip Proverbs for Today?' I sighed. 'You'll be on to stitches in time saving nine next.'

'There's a much more appropriate one, matey.'

'Is there?'

'Don't make waves.'

I took the point and retreated into an aggrieved silence but it did not last long. The car turned in through some wrought-iron gates and went down a wide drive. As the vehicle pulled up for us to get out, a bevy of press photographers converged with cameras at the ready.

Clive gave me an encouraging nudge.

'Watch the birdie—and smile!'

◇◇◇

Shohei Ogino was waiting for us in the clubhouse with his three sons, his senior management team and a highly select band of close friends and business colleagues. The tableau was arranged in strict hierarchical order with Ogino himself at the centre. At this—our first meeting—he made sure that I came to him as if paying allegiance to some medieval overlord and the event was duly recorded on the video camera that was strategically placed in a corner. Standing beside the cameraman was an attractive young Japanese woman in designer denim and cap. Chiyo Takumi did not seem at all abashed to be the only female in the room.

'Welcome to my country,' said Shohei Ogino.

'Thanks,' I said, shaking the proffered hand. 'It's very kind of you to invite me. I'm delighted to be here.'

'The pleasure is ours.'

He gave me a little bow but I was not fooled by the excessive courtesy of his manner. Shohei Ogino was made out of pure steel. Short, trim and erect in a beautifully cut dark blue suit, he almost glowed with power and everyone around him stood in attitudes of respect. The face was large and the laser-beam eyes were protected behind a pair of gold-framed spectacles. A high forehead gave way to sparse grey hair that was carefully slicked down. He appraised me in a second and was satisfied with what he saw. Clive then went through the handshake routine before our host made the introductions. Ogino's Rolex watch glinted as his arm moved.

'Here are my sons—Takeshi, Yasayuki and Fumio.'

It was easy to pick out the golfer. Apart from being by far the youngest—early twenties at most—he was the only man who had spurned the standard business suit. Dressed in shirt, slacks and a Pringle sweater, he was beaming away with the rest of them but he was also sizing me up as his father had done. He was of middle height with broad shoulders and narrow hips. His black hair was styled like that of a pop singer and there was a glamour-boy sparkle to him. His elder brothers, by contrast, Takeshi and Yasayuki, were clones of their father with identical expressions on their faces. I could guess what Fumio Ogino was thinking and sense the hesitant blend of hostility and distant envy, but the two brothers had smiles that were quite impenetrable.

Clive and I pumped hands as the rollcall was made.

'This is Seizo Togawa…and Eishi Sasaki…my good friend, Akio Ushiba…Michizo Yamada…Shintaro Masuda…and this is my esteemed colleague…'

I tried hard to memorise the names but they all merged together in a meaningless blur. The important people were the family—Shohei Ogino and his three sons. Chiyo Takumi would be a difficult person to forget in the circumstances and our friendship was sealed when she shot me a smile of sympathy before moving her cameramen to a new vantage point.

'And now,' said Ogino. 'We will go outside…'

The crowd parted for him to lead the way. I went into the locker room and changed quickly into my golf attire with Clive hissing orders into my ear. He also took time off to pass a few lecherous remarks about our film director and to wonder if she had any special skills with croissant or banana. It does not take much to kick-start the motor of his desire and it was soon roaring away merrily. I was more concerned with getting through the ritual that lay ahead. My idea of making an instructional video was to have a club, a golf ball and a camera. That was all. Who needed the assembled journos and a representative cross-section of the business world of Tokyo? I was being over-sold.

'On the tee, Alan Saxon…'

Clive got a laugh with his announcement as I stepped up to address my ball. It was not the best drive that I've ever hit but it went straight down the fairway. Photographers flashed away,

the video camera rolled and the audience, which had been aug-
mented by curious club members, gave me a round of applause.
I hit another half-dozen balls before I began to loosen up and
find the right tempo. Over twenty had been dispatched up into
the blue sky before the publicity machine had had its fill. But
the show was not yet over.

'On the tee, Fumio Ogino…'

It was the proud father himself making the announcement
this time. His youngest son, now clad entirely in black, came
up to me and offered his hand but it was no greeting that we
exchanged. It was the token gesture between two boxers before
they try to pound each other into the canvas. Fumio Ogino was
not there to congratulate me on my skill with the driver. He was
out to surpass it and to put me in my place.

The partisan spectators gave his first soaring shot a mild ova-
tion and his father nodded with quiet satisfaction. He repeated
his triumph nine more times. Fumio Ogino was good. Strong,
well-balanced and wristy, he had developed a swing that was
both effective and eye-catching with a smooth pivotal action and
an explosive contact with the ball. His direction was sometimes
awry but he averaged at least thirty or forty yards more than I
had managed. As the clapping intensified, he stepped back and
indicated that I should take over again but I shook my head and
smiled. I felt like an old gunfighter who has been set up to fight
a duel in the sun with the latest young desperado to learn how
to fire a gun. Fumio Ogino was not going to use me to advance
his burgeoning reputation. With a comical gesture, I pretended
to concede defeat and laughter brought the exhibition to an end.
My challenger was pleased by what he saw as a minor victory
but annoyed to be cheated out of greater honours.

Shohei Ogino thanked everyone for coming and the party
began to break up. Clive Phelps patted me on the back.

'Well done, Saxon. Poetry in motion.'

'I could've done without Junior stealing my thunder.'

'Too flashy for my liking.'

'No wonder Sam Limsong has a thing about him.'

'Yes. Fumio gets to you, doesn't he?'

'His father sprung him on me before I could object.'

'Easy to see which is the favourite son,' said Clive with a glance at the other two contenders. 'Shohei launched him like some new product. The latest piece of electronic wizardry from the Ogino factories. Flick the switch and you get all those pyrotechnics from Tokyo Action Man.'

'I think the kid just wanted to prove a point.'

Chiyo Takumi came over to introduce herself properly to us and she endured Clive's lingering handshake without undue embarrassment. There was a freewheeling confidence about her which turned a handsome woman into a very tempting one and I knew that I would have to restrain my colleague. When she fixed her dark eyes on me, I found myself wondering if I might be in need of restraint myself. Chiyo had a very special quality. A classic Japanese face was subtly altered by her contact with the West. Her relaxed manner was a boon after the feet-together formality of the business community.

'That was a great performance, Alan,' she said.

'Thanks.'

'Pity that Fumio horned in. He ruined things.'

'His admirers didn't think so.'

'Oh, he's got talent,' she conceded, 'but he's still very raw. Your swing is beautiful. So stylish. It will be a privilege to capture it on film. Fumio can hit the ball a long way but he has no real class. You have.'

'Keep talking,' I said, warming to her.

'I intend to—over dinner. We have a lot to discuss.'

'Your place or ours?' asked Clive.

'Yours. Eight o'clock?'

'Done,' I said.

Restored by her comments, I went back to the locker room to change then joined the stragglers in the clubhouse. Clive was chatting to Shohei Ogino with the two somnolent elder sons in attendance. There was no sign of my young rival. I was about to cross to the bar to get a drink when I was accosted by someone who saved me the trouble. A stocky man of middle height and middle years handed me a glass of orange juice and chuckled. I'd noticed him during the first round of introductions because his handshake had been very firm and he was animated by good humour.

'Thanks,' I said. 'Just what I needed.'

'You do not like to drink too much alcohol.'

'How do you know that?'

'I have read your book,' he said. 'And I am hoping that you will be so kind as to sign it for me.'

'Of course.'

'I will bring it along some time.'

'Did you enjoy reading it?'

'Oh, yes. I laughed a lot.'

The ripe chuckle made him rock slightly and an uneven row of teeth appeared in the middle of the flabby face. His easy joviality was a tonic in itself. Though grammatically correct, his English had a thick accent.

'I am Akio Ushiba,' he said.

'Do you work for Mr Ogino?'

'From time to time. We are also close friends.'

'Are you a golfer yourself?'

'Only a poor amateur. But I try, Alan, I try.'

'Are you a member here?'

'At Wada?' He shook with mirth. 'I would be bankrupt if I tried to join a club like this. Do you know how much the annual club membership is here?'

'Pretty steep, I suppose.'

'£300,000.'

'Wow!'

'That would leave a big hole in my salary. In fact, it would be all hole and no salary.' He guffawed at his little joke. 'Even in Japan, very few individuals have that kind of money to spend on golf so memberships tend to be corporate. Shohei's company has invested heavily in Wada International Country Club. I play here when my friend invites me.'

'What are the green fees?'

'£1000 for a morning's golf.'

'How can *anybody* afford that?'

'It's a kind of madness, isn't it,' he said. 'If the golf courses back in Leicester had charged that much, we would have had no Alan Saxon, I think.'

'Dead right, Mr Ushiba.'

'In your book, you say you paid next to nothing.'

'That was on the local Pitch and Putt course,' I explained. 'But even a full round of golf would only cost a couple of quid in those days. That's two pounds.'

'What a wonderful country!'

'It has its attractions.' I took a sip from my orange juice. 'On the other hand, it has its less attractive sides.'

'Your father is one of them.'

'What?'

'You do not have to hide it from me, my friend. I could read it between the lines of your story. Why else did you say so little about Tom Saxon? As soon as your career takes off, he disappears altogether.'

'That's...just the way it happened.'

'Didn't he like golf?'

'Hated it.'

'He tried to stop you playing it, then?'

'All the time,' I recalled. 'Rugby was his game. Loved all that violence. He was in the Police XV for years as a second row—that's one of the forwards.'

'I know. We have rugby in this country, too.'

'My father never forgave me for not enjoying rugby. He expected me to get into the school team. It was a test of manhood to me and I failed.' I shrugged sadly. 'That's where it all started, I'm afraid. Then it went from bad to worse.'

'Do you despise him?'

'Let's just say that we don't get on.'

'Is it because he was a policeman?'

'Partly that.'

'Someone has to do the job.'

'That's what he always says.'

His mobile face was quiescent for once as he pondered.

'It is a tragedy,' he said at length. 'If you had understood his way of life, maybe he would have understood yours a bit better. A father is a father, Alan. He must take some pleasure out of your achievements.'

'I doubt it.'

'Did you send him a copy of your book?'

'No,' I confessed. 'But he bought one himself.'

'There you are…'

Someone joined us and began talking to my companion in Japanese. The chuckle came back then Akio Ushiba waved an apology to me and he moved away to hear more. A country club in Tokyo was the last place I'd expected to be talking about my father, least of all so openly, but there was something unusual about Ushiba. His amiability was quite disarming. I had felt no pain while telling him some bitter truths.

Shohei Ogino came across to take his leave and I collected yet another handshake and bow. Everything had gone as he had decreed and he was palpably delighted. All three sons were now at his shoulder with Fumio subduing his aggression beneath a show of filial respect. Relieved to have come through my audition, I chatted happily with my host for a few minutes and I was getting on extremely well.

In one sentence, I sabotaged all my good work.

'By the way,' I said, 'Sam Limsong sends his regards.'

His eyes blazed behind his spectacles. Though iron self-control remained, he was profoundly insulted. After giving me a final bow, he made a dignified exit with his two elder sons trailing behind him. Fumio Ogino stayed long enough to try his broken English out on me.

'You be sorry for that.'

He meant it.

Chapter Four

Clive Phelps was not a man to mince his words. The drive back to the Imperial Hotel was in the nature of a sustained tirade against me. Separated from the chauffeur by a sound-proofed screen and accorded a double layer of privacy by the man's total ignorance of our language, Clive felt able to give his disgust free rein.

'Have you taken leave of your tiny fucking mind?'

'It was only a casual remark.'

'Casual remark!' he yelled. 'Christ Almighty, man! Have you any idea how difficult it was to set this deal up? It took me six months of hard bloody graft. I mean, this could've been a dream assignment. Money for old rope. And what happens? You tie that old rope round our necks!'

'Look, it wasn't deliberate.'

'Alan Saxon. Our ambassador in Japan.'

'Clive…'

'Why not go the whole hog and remind him who won the last war. Why not throw in a few gags about the new Emperor? Why not tell him that all Japs look alike to you?'

'You're over-reacting.'

'I'm *entitled* to over-react.'

'It just slipped out.'

'It always does.'

'Mr Ogino will soon forget it.'

'He's Japanese. They have memories like elephants.'

'Then we simply have to rise above it.'

'Listen to him, will you!' howled Clive. 'You bury us to our neck in shit then tell me to rise above it! Don't make waves, I said. Don't make sodding waves! So you go ahead and create a typhoon.'

I let him sound off for another five minutes without interruption then I waited for a convenient pause. When it came, I slipped in what I thought was a reasonable comment.

'Sam Limsong was right about one thing.'

'Don't mention that Asiatic excrescence!'

'You have to be careful with Ogino.'

'*Now* he tells me!'

'He takes offence so easily.'

'Only when some congenital imbecile provokes him.'

'There has to be a reason for it.'

'Your mother probably smoked during pregnancy. The size of your brain was severely diminished.'

'A reason why Ogino has it in for Sam Limsong, I mean.'

'Who the hell cares?'

'It's not only because of that youngest son.'

'Saxon…'

'There's something else. Something deeper.'

'All I'm interested in is survival,' said Clive through gritted teeth. 'You play a round of golf in Thailand and a fortnight's holiday in Japan is ruined. Why couldn't you just go to Bangkok to get laid like the rest of us? If you'd spent an hour with Banana Woman instead of a morning with Sam Limsong, we'd actually be having some fun now.'

'The situation can be retrieved.'

'I hope so,' he said grimly. 'I hope so.'

'We just have to make a cracking video for him.'

'On what? The Lost Art of Diplomacy?'

'Fences can always be mended.'

'Not when *you've* knocked them down.'

'I'll be a model of tact and discretion from now on.'

Sardonic laughter filled the rear of the car.

◇◇◇

Time may not heal all wounds but it can certainly take the sting out of them. Several drinks and a couple of hours away from me worked their magic on Clive. Though he was still seething with anger underneath, he was now able to manage a token civility. The prospect of dinner with the delectable Chiyo Takumi also had a calming effect. After a shower and a change of clothes, he was almost sociable again, rationing his expletives to a mere one per sentence. Since there were thirteen restaurants at the hotel, he gave himself the task of touring them all in order to find the one most suitable for what he was evidently seeing as a kind of tryst. By the time that Chiyo actually turned up, Clive was beginning to enjoy himself but that enjoyment was instantly smothered when he saw that she had brought a man with her. A sense of betrayal made him splutter helplessly.

'Now that's not bloody fair!'

'She's trying to tell you something, Clive.'

'Who is he? Husband? Lover? Friend?'

'Bodyguard,' I said. 'Your reputation went before you.'

Hope stirred. 'I suppose he could be her brother.'

Hideo Nakane was none of these things. Tall, slim and smiling, he was the translator who would be working on the Japanese commentary for the instructional video. He was still in his twenties but his faintly academic air made him seem older. Clive warmed to him at once when he realised that there was no romantic interest between our two guests and I responded to the man's soft-edged geniality.

'Feel free to use me at any time,' he said. 'Japan can be very confusing to the foreign visitor. Let me be your interpreter. If you have any problems with our language, just give me a call.'

'Thanks,' I said. 'I'll do that.'

'Your problems are with the *English* language,' noted Clive in a barbed aside. 'Why not take a vow of silence for the next two weeks and save us all a lot of trouble?'

We adjourned to the restaurant and ordered drinks while we consulted the menu. Chiyo was wearing a blue silk trouser suit that showed off her figure to more effect than her film director's denim. Hideo wore a dark grey suit with a bold pinstripe and a red silk tie. Both were at once relaxed and businesslike, ready to enjoy the occasion to the full without losing sight of the fact that there was work to do. When the food had been ordered, we raised our glasses to toast the success of our enterprise.

'How are you finding the Imperial?' said Chiyo.

'No complaints so far,' I replied.

'Apart from one thing,' said Clive with mock outrage. 'There were no suits in my room.'

'Suits?' she repeated.

'Yes,' he said. 'I was looking at this half-page advert in the English Telephone Directory. It's right there in black and white. "Imperial Hotel. Accommodation Facilities. 1,140 rooms, 76 suits." When I opened my wardrobe, there wasn't a suit in sight!'

We all laughed at the misprint, then Clive stroked his moustache and went straight into his chat-up routine.

'And where are you staying, Chiyo?' he purred.

'At the New Otani.'

'I've always wanted to see inside there...'

Hideo Nakane was amused at the by-play and let them get on with it. I took the opportunity to find out a little more about the Ogino family.

'We met Fumio this afternoon,' I observed.

'So I hear. What did you think of him?'

'He can certainly hit a golf ball.'

'As a person, I meant.'

'Talented but obnoxious.'

His quiet chuckle confirmed that I had found a true friend. Hideo Nakane did not feel the need to kowtow to the Ogino dynasty like all the others I had met. He was his own man. His grasp of English was outstanding and his accent was all but faultless. I pressed for more details.

'How good a golfer is he?'

'Three wins this season on the Japanese circuit and respectable finishes in most other tournaments. Fumio's potential is unlimited. I saw him beat Sam Limsong in a play-off at Kasumi-gaseki earlier this year and he was in superlative form that day.' He looked across at me. 'I'm surprised you haven't seen mentions of Fumio in any of your golf magazines.'

'I never read them. They say nasty things about me.'

His eyes twinkled. 'Especially after your book.'

'I had to get my revenge somehow.'

'Coming back to Fumio…'

'Please do.'

'We won't know how good he really is until he plays on the U.S.P.G.A Tour next year. But the portents are very encouraging. Yokuri Tanizaki has predicated that our new star could go right to the top.'

There was no better recommendation than that. Tanizaki was an old adversary of mine, a brilliant golfer with a short game that could take the heart out of his playing partners. Monster putts and chips on to the green from impossible lines were his speciality. If *he* was praising Fumio Ogino, then the young man certainly had a future in the game. To that end, the father's influence was vital.

'It means a lot to Shohei, doesn't it?' I said.

'It means everything,' explained Hideo. 'He's invested a fortune in Fumio's career but the emotional investment is even greater. It would be the happiest day in his life if his youngest son could win a Major.'

'And what about his other sons?'

'What about them?'

'Would they be equally delighted?'

Hideo glanced at Chiyo to make sure that she was not listening, then he lowered his voice.

'They will be very pleased, of course. It will bring great honour to the family and all will share in the reflected glory.' He paused then shrugged. 'That is what will happen in public at all events.'

'And in private?'

'Takeshi and Yasayuki will have reservations.'

'They don't like their brother?'

'They love him as they have been brought up to do.'

'But they resent their father for favouritising him.'

'Perhaps that is so. Who knows?'

'Tell me some more about them.'

'Takeshi has great managerial skills,' he said, 'and he will, in time, succeed his father and run the Ogino empire. He models himself on Shohei and wants nothing more than the chance to emulate him.'

'What about Yasayuki?'

'He is the most interesting of the three in some ways. Yasa-yuki is certainly the brightest. He should be. He's a graduate of Tsukuba.'

'Where's that?'

Surprise registered. 'You've never heard of Tsukuba?'

'The only places I know about in Japan are the golf courses. We're an ignorant lot in this game, Hideo. We charge round the globe but see little more of it than the next eighteen holes. Golf narrows the mind.'

'Tsukuba is Science City.'

'Come again.'

'It's some sixty kilometres north of Tokyo and it's probably the most intelligent city on earth.' He smiled at my cynical reaction. 'That's no boast, Alan. Look at the external evidence. Science City has two universities, over fifty national research institutes and a population that includes seven thousand doctorates.'

'You can't say that about Leicester!' I admitted.

'They began to build Tsukuba in the late 1950s. Its aim was to revolutionise and internationalise Japanese science.' There was the merest hint of disapproval. 'I think it has delivered the goods, don't you?'

'In triplicate. And Yasayuki went there?'

'His doctoral thesis was on some branch of electronic sur-veillance. Its findings have been have put to sound commercial use by the Ogino Corporation.'

'How does Yasayuki get on with Takeshi?' I said.

'They are brothers.'

'Rivals, too, I suspect.'

Hideo Nakane gave a non-committal shrug. The food then arrived and the conversation opened out to include the others. Chiyo had obviously had no difficulty in keeping Clive's rampant libido at bay but he had not abandoned hopes. For the time being, however, business called. Over tasty and exquisitely presented Japanese cuisine, we reviewed the task ahead of us. Clive and I had already had several meetings back in Britain to agree on the main lines of our approach and his script was a working summary of those meetings. Chiyo Takumi had transformed it. Reading it with the eye of a director, she had reshaped it expertly to get maximum dramatic value. When she gave us each a copy of her camera script, the whole project took on a new excitement. I'd come to take part in an instructional video and now found myself starring in a feature film. Move over, Clint.

Our translator had his Japanese version of the script and aimed a stream of queries at Chiyo. Like her, he was a consummate professional. They brought out the best in Clive Phelps who suggested experiments and refinements that we might try. I chipped in the odd comment but was a fascinated spectator for most of the time. By the end of the meal, I was in a state of exhilaration. The tense moment with Shohei Ogino had faded into the back of my mind but it was still a dull ache and so I decided to confide in Hideo Nakane. Here, after all, was a culture clash that needed to be resolved. I waited till our guests were leaving then fell in beside him. While Clive was making his last bid for an invitation to view Tokyo from the window of a room at the New Otani, I gave Hideo a brief description of what had happened at the Wada International Country Club. Since I would be meeting the family again on the following evening, I was anxious to know the protocol.

'Do you think I should apologise to Shohei?'

'No, Alan,' he said. 'Put it right behind you.'

'I feel that I should say something.'

'It's too late, my friend.'

'Why?'

'*He o hitte shiri tsubome.*'

'What's that?'

'An old Japanese proverb.'

'Meaning?'

'No use scrunching up your buttocks after a fart.'

I got the message.

◇◇◇

There were many positives on which to reflect as I lay in the bath that night. Both Chiyo and Hideo had proved their worth and it would be a pleasure to work alongside them. The sheer scale of the venture had become clearer to me. My moment of glory on screen was being marketed for worldwide distribution. Hideo was responsible for the Japanese version, in which my own voice would be dubbed by a local actor, but other countries would benefit from my sage advice as well. Alan Saxon would speak in several languages before he had finished. A lifetime's experience would be crystallised into an hour's footage. I would play a series of superb shots because anything less than perfection would be carefully edited out. It would be sunshine all the way with no shadows on the grass.

Hideo's comments on the Ogino family had been highly illuminating. Only the rich could play on a golf course in Japan and only the mega-rich could subsidise their son's ambitions to have a professional career. Fumio's undoubted talent and his father's unquestioned influence had already put the young man's face on the covers of golf magazines in the Far East. In five years' time—if all went to plan—it would be Fumio Ogino who was making an instructional video. I fought hard against the inevitable feelings of resentment as I looked back over the long struggles to establish myself in the professional ranks. Akio Ushiba had been right. It would all have been so much easier with financial backing and parental support.

A gruesome thought intruded. My video would be marketed in Britain in due course and feed the hopes of many would-be golfers. It would also be available to others who might have a personal interest. I had visions of my father, opening his Christmas present from Dorothy and finding that it was a message from his son in Japan. The idea made me shudder. He would have me on tape whenever he wanted, able to start and stop me at will. The pointing finger of Tom Saxon had controlled my childhood with crude authority. It would soon be able to bring me to life again or kill me at a touch. All of a sudden, the water in the bath felt cold.

Tense and unable to sleep, I did something that I've never done before. In the hope that it might ease mind and body, I dialled Reception and ordered a massage. Clive Phelps had recommended it to me, having tried it himself on arrival. Gravely disappointed when they sent up a young man instead of a sensuous Geisha girl with six-inch fingernails, he was soon won over by the alternative technique of the masseur. It sounded as if it might be just the thing that I needed.

I did not have long to wait. There was a tap on the door and I opened it to admit a lithe young man with a crew-cut. Dressed in what looked like judo attire, he had slippers on his feet and carried a sponge bag. He bowed, announced his name, put the DO NOT DISTURB sign on the outside of my door then came in. My experience with masseurs is not wide. Most of the breed that I've encountered have been burly men with bulging forearms who attack my body as if trying to reshape it into a more acceptable form. This was quite different.

I was standing there in my pyjamas and assumed that he would like me to wear nothing more than a towel around my waist. When I began to undo the buttons, however, he held up his hands in horror as if I was turning into a werewolf.

'No! No! Please—wait!'

He ran to my wardrobe and searched it for a few moments until he found what he wanted. It was a cotton kimono folded over and kept in a plastic bag. He handed it to me with mimed instructions, then turned his back so that I could strip off and slip the garment on.

'First time?' he said.

'Yes.'

'Japanese massage?'

'Please.'

'Oil? Powder?'

'No thanks.'

He asked me to lie on my side on the bed then kicked off his slippers before climbing up beside me. Taking a small square of cloth from his bag, he positioned himself so that he could get at me, starting with my neck and my shoulders. Everything was done with thumb pressure through the fabric. At no point did he make direct contact with my skin. He explored and kneaded my neck in a way that left me stranded somewhere between pain and pleasure, forcing down hard on stiff muscles in order to release their tension. Ten minutes or more were spent on what he identified immediately as the problem area. He then moved on to the head itself, using fingers and thumbs to probe and test then lightly smacking my cranium by way of stimulation. My right arm was next in line for treatment and had to be covered with his little cloth before he could begin.

When he turned his attention to my back, he pushed down his thumb harder then ever on a series of thirteen pressure points up and down my spine. He was finding muscles that I did not even know had existed and which came alive to register a protest at the searching hands. He made me turn over on my other side so he could repeat the process on the upper half of my torso. It was manipulation rather than the sadistic pummelling to which I have been subjected to on other massage tables and it was strangely liberating. Once the pain ebbed away, it left the muscles feeling soft and warm.

The next test of endurance was to lie face down while he worked on the backs of my legs and my feet, then he flipped me over like a pancake before addressing my chest. When the massage was complete, he jumped off the bed, put his feet together and bowed politely.

'Thank you. Goodbye.'

He was gone before I could find enough strength to find some money to tip him. I lay there feeling as if my whole body had been taken expertly apart before being thoroughly cleaned and reassembled again. My mind had been freed from its cloying anxieties. I was floating. A lazy arm snaked out to switch off the bedside lamp, then I had the best night of sleep for weeks.

◇◇◇

Chiyo Takumi and her film crew were waiting for us when we arrived at the golf course next morning. There were two cameramen and a sound technician, all male, and a tiny girl with a clipboard who turned out to be Chiyo's personal assistant. Expensive-looking equipment stood ready near the practice area and I saw that the Ogino logo was on every item. Having been filmed with his own video cameras, we would be processed in the company laboratories. Something else was waiting for us and it sparked me off at once.

'What's that, Clive?' I demanded.

'A golf bag.'

'I have clubs of my own.'

'But they weren't made by the sponsor.'

'They're the ones I'm going to use.'

'Be reasonable, Saxon.'

'I did not bring them all the way from England to sit in my bag.'

'Save them for the odd round with the corporate execs.'

'No!'

'Jesus wept!' he sighed. 'I knew you'd be difficult.'

It was the reason he had concealed the truth from me until the last moment so that he could confront me with a *fait accompli*. My clubs are very dear to me, beloved tools of the trade that have served me well over the years and endured countless visits to the repair shop. Since the time when they were stolen from my hotel bedroom in Sydney on one occasion—then happily recovered—I've hardly let them out of my sight. No Japanese club manufacturer was going to separate me from my faithful old putter. It would be worse than amputation.

Hideo Nakane came to the rescue. Walking in on the scene and understanding the problem at once, he suggested the ideal compromise. The shining white bag with its name emblazoned in red could stand in the background on its golf cart for every shot. Its fourteen brand new clubs would remain untouched. Though pretending to advertise a leading manufacturer in the field, I would instead be using my own clubs. Honour was satisfied all round. Our sponsor might object if he knew what was happening but the magic of film would pull the wool over his eyes.

'Let's get started,' said Chiyo.

'Where do you want me?' I asked.

'Sitting down so the Keiko can reach you.'

'Why?'

I soon found out. The diminutive Keiko was doubling as a make-up girl. Getting me to sit on a folding stool, she stood over me and used a hairbrush to tidy my errant locks. She also applied some colour to my cheeks and eyebrows then powdered me gently down. Her deft fingers straightened the collar on my shirt.

'Wear this every day,' she ordered.

'What?'

'Continuity.'

'Yes,' added Chiyo. 'We can't have you hitting tee shots in that blue shirt, getting out of a bunker in a red one then putting in a different colour again. Two weeks of filming must look like one complete round of golf.'

'You take shirt off later,' said Keiko. 'I wash.'

'Every day?'

'I keep it clean.'

'Will you take *my* shirt off as well?' asked Clive.

Keiko giggled and picked up her clipboard.

Chiyo took control and the next couple of hours flashed by without much to show for them. I had no idea how long it took to rehearse a sequence and line up a camera shot. Chiyo was a perfectionist. When I used my driver—apparently plucked from the golf bag behind me—she filmed me from a series of different angles so that the mechanics of the swing could be clearly demonstrated. One of the cameramen was even sent a few hundred yards away so that his zoom lens could pick me up from a frontal position, then follow the flight of the ball as it soared through the air. My best tee shot of all was far too accurate and sent him scampering for his life as if came out of the sky at him like a bullet. It gave us a good laugh and a cue to break for refreshments.

Hideo and Clive weighed in with praise and much-needed reassurance. They would not add their commentary until a later stage when they would work in the comparative comfort of a recording studio and not have to bother about which shirt they were wearing and how their hair looked.

'It'll take us *months* at this rate,' I said.

'The first day is always the worst,' said Chiyo. 'We're bound to have teething troubles. We may only be able to use a minute or two of what we have so far but it's a start.'

'Why did you stop me halfway through?'

'A cloud drifted across the sun and the quality of the light changed. These things are all important, Alan.'

'To the people who'll buy the video?'

'To me.'

We resumed our work and made slightly better progress but it was obviously going to be a long haul. While I sympathised with the technical problems, I was more concerned with my own difficulty in maintaining concentration and tempo. The stop-start nature of the work was not fertile ground for vintage Alan Saxon but I persevered. Lunch was followed by another couple of hours until our lighting director slowly began to dim his lamps in the sky. Hideo helped me to load the two golf bags into the boot of our limousine. His presence had been invaluable throughout.

'See you tonight, then, Alan,' he said.

'What sort of a party is it?'

'Very low-key. Nothing riotous.'

'How many will be there?'

'Forty or fifty, maybe.'

'Will Shohei speak to me?'

'Of course. He'll be the soul of courtesy. I'll tell him how well everything went today. That'll soothe him.'

'Thanks.'

Clive and I evaluated our first day as we were driven back towards the city. He was full of admiration but it was all targeted on Chiyo and her directorial flair. I fished for compliments that did not come so I became more direct.

'What about *me*?'

'Your make-up was terrific.'

'Is that all you can say?'

'Lovely wig-join as well.'

We parted as we came out of the hotel lift and the porter trolleyed the two golf bags into my room. Left alone to examine them more carefully, I had to admit how much smarter the new one was. My own bag was wrinkled with age and scuffed with long usage. Every time I took it off the carousel at an airport, it had acquired fresh wounds in transit. Baggage handlers lack the gentle touch. As I stacked the two sets of clubs side by side, I realised the stupidity of lugging both to and from the course each day. Since the sponsor's name was paramount, it would be more sensible for me to keep my own clubs in his bag, then pull them out as I needed them as if they were truly the brand I was supposed to be advertising. I implemented my decision at once, taking out my own set one by one and laying them on the bed. It was when I stood my bag too robustly on its end that I heard the click. Something had fallen down inside.

I shook the bag and the rattle was distinct. Upending it over the bed, I was amazed when a small, round metallic object dropped down among my clubs. It was not much bigger than a pound coin in circumference though it was a lot thicker. As I lifted it up between two fingers, it brushed the shaft of my 9-iron and clung to it tenaciously. I grabbed my golf bag again and looked inside it. A third of the way down was a steel band for reinforcement. Plucking the magnetised object from its mooring, I stuck it instead on the steel band where it held fast. When my clubs had been slotted into position, they would have pushed a padded lining against the wall of the bag and kept the magnet even more securely in position. But for the need to use the sponsor's golf bag, I would never have found the intruder.

Putting it in the palm of my hand, I held it up to the light to examine it more closely. The Ogino logo was franked clearly on the shiny surface of the metal and that confirmed my suspicion. The feeling of unease which had troubled me in a Bangkok hotel and during a Thai International flight now returned once again with greater intensity. There was no doubt about the object which I had accidentally discovered.

It was a bugging device.

Chapter Five

Property values in central Tokyo are so astronomically high that its citizens have been driven further and further out into its sprawling suburbs. To own an apartment in the heart of the city argues real money, but to possess a large house requires substantial wealth. The Ogino residence was a long, low, two-storey building less than ten minutes by car from our hotel. It was impossible to see anything in the darkness beyond its bare outline but that gave a sense of power and stability. The opulent interior recorded the same message at full volume. Shohei Ogino had little time for the customary frugalities in the Japanese mode. The spacious living room was filled with expensive Western-style furniture that was set off by some spectacular *objets d'art*. Though the atmosphere was quintessentially Oriental, the decor would have passed muster in Knightsbridge.

Clive Phelps, Chiyo Takumi and I were guests of honour at the party which let us in for another testing round of hand-shakes. There were some forty or so people present, all the men in suits and most of the women in cocktail dresses. A few of the women, however, favoured traditional attire and one of these was Masako Ogino, wife of Shohei and mother of his three sons. She was a short and rather plump woman with lustrous black hair that had been carefully back-combed and pinned up with an array of elaborate slides. The face had an almost Geisha white-ness to it and vestiges of her former beauty were still plentiful. Shohei stood beside her at all times as he dispensed smiles and pleasantries to friends and colleagues alike. He was plainly revelling in the role of husband and father, which was something that had never even occurred to a certain policeman in Leicestershire. By the same token, it had never occurred to me to be as respectful towards my father as Takeshi, Yasayuki and Fumio.

The real find of the evening was Mitsu. Nobody had told me that Shohei had a daughter as well or that she was so gorgeous. She was an interesting blend of her parents with her mother's handsomeness and her father's cool intensity. Mitsu Ogino had a tinkling laugh that was all her own and I tried to generate as much as I could of it. She was wearing a black silk sheath dress with patterned dragons on it and sipping some warm *sake*.

'Father has talked much about you, Mr Saxon,' she said.

'The nice things were all true.'

'There were lots of them.'

'Tell me. Very slowly.'

The tinkling laugh. 'It would take too long.'

'I'm a good listener.'

Mitsu had an effervescence that reminded me in a peculiar way of my late Aunt Enid. It was a sort of unquenchable love of life that went its own way without any deference to those around her. She had none of the cowed obedience shown by her elder brothers nor yet the bumptious arrogance of Fumio. There was a ready explanation.

'I spent a year in America.'

'Which part?'

'Boston. I studied at Harvard Business School.'

'Why there?'

'I had to get away from Japan,' she said levelly. 'A woman's role is very restricted here. We are educated into submission and acceptance. I wanted to strike out on my own. I wanted more freedom.'

'You sound like my daughter.'

'Is she a student?'

'At school in England,' I said fondly. 'Lynette is always talking about bucking the system and making her escape. I pity her teachers, honestly. She takes after me. Lynette is a natural boat-rocker.'

'Boat-rocker? I do not know this word.'

'Someone who rocks the boat. A rebel. An awkwardee.'

'A person who likes to cause a disturbance.'

'Yes,' I said. 'Who upsets the status quo. Someone who refuses to stay in line. You're a boat-rocker yourself.'

'Me?' The notion made her giggle.

'Well, you're no tame conformist. Most people obey the rules simply because they're there. You change them. You want some control over your own destiny.'

'Which is not easy in this country. Look at them.'

'Who?'

'The other women present.'

I saw what she meant. Almost all of the ladies were listening to men in an attitude of deference. Even Chiyo was subdued and respectful in the family home as she played a social game she had been taught from infancy. In a gathering like that, none of the women dared to rock the boat.

'Language is the key,' said Mitsu. 'It is the mirror of our culture. When you speak to someone, his or her sex, age and status must be evident in the words you use and the way you say them. Our language is full of subtle barriers and signposts of rank. Women come off worst. We have to use our own vocabulary full of polite pronouns and endless courtesies. I hate that kind of Women's Japanese.'

'How does your father react to that?' I said.

'He is coming to understand me.'

'Did he mind you going abroad to study?'

'Father encouraged it.'

'What was Boston like?'

'I loved it.'

'Would you like to go back there?'

She frowned for a second then gave me her laugh again. I was about to press for more details when her mother waved Mitsu over to her. As I watched the girl go, Clive Phelps sidled up to whisper in my ear.

'Hands off!' he warned. 'She's Ogino's daughter.'

'We were just chatting.'

'You were grinning at her, you idiot. That constitutes statutory rape in the minds of the Old Guard. We're here to palliate Shohei not to stir him up even more.'

'He was charming to me when we arrived.'

'Window-dressing.'

'Shohei doesn't hold any grudges.'

'Don't bet on it.'

'The whole family have given me a warm welcome.'

'Make sure it doesn't turn sour this time,' said Clive. 'Now, listen carefully. Shohei is bound to want a word alone with you at some stage so be tactful. Got it? Very tactful.'

'I promise not to make any references to the Bridge on the River Kwai,' I teased. 'I'll just whistle the Colonel Bogey March to show him there are no hard feelings.'

'Keep your voice down.'

'Trust me, Clive. I've learned my lesson.'

'Don't make waves.'

'I'll pour oil on troubled water instead.'

'That'll be the day!'

Clive was distracted by one of the waitresses who was cruising around with trays of nibbles. While he helped himself to a slice of *sushi*, I looked around for a friendly face. I was hoping to see Akio Ushiba again because I'd enjoyed our earlier meeting but there was no sign of him. Chiyo was deep in conversation with two women and Hideo was talking to Takeshi Ogino. The latter was much more relaxed on his home ground and the deadpan face was now quite animated. Takeshi had his father's gestures and something of his autocratic stance. It was almost as if he were rehearsing to take over the part. Hideo Nakane was showing him all due deference.

My interest shifted to Yasayuki Ogino, the second of the three sons, who was talking to a rather distinguished-looking older man. I could see what Hideo had meant about Yasayuki's intelligence. It shone out of him. Caught up in a discussion that clearly fired him, he was gesticulating with his hands and nodding urgently away. His eyes were alight with the half-madness of the true scientist and it was easy to imagine him dominating a seminar during his days at Tsukuba. Qualities which had remained hidden at our first encounter now revealed themselves. The intelligence was allied to an assertive and almost peremptory manner which was further buttressed by the quiet frenzy of a man who believes himself to be absolutely in the right. Watching him was intriguing until I recalled the subject of his doctorial thesis.

It was electronic surveillance.

'Mr Saxon...?'

'Oh, hello.'

'You like party?'

'Yes, very much. I'm enjoying every moment.'

'Welcome to house.'

'Thank you.'

'Nice see you again.'

Fumio Ogino was struggling with words that sounded as if they had been practised in front of a mirror. A smile was in place on his lips but it could never reach his eyes. I had the feeling that he was trying to make amends for the warning he had given me in the clubhouse and I was grateful for that, but I did not let myself be taken in by the surface politeness. Fumio still saw me as a rival.

'I watch play,' he said.

'Did you?'

'Singapore Open. Five years, I think.'

'Six, actually,' I corrected. 'I never forget any of my tournament wins. They don't come round that often.'

'You play well.'

'Thanks.'

'I like way you attack. Go for flag.'

'Percentage golf is not my scene, Fumio. When all's said and done, we're entertainers. Play safe all the time and we bore the paying audience.'

'My father like your style.'

'That's very kind of him.'

'He want me be Alan Saxon of Japan.'

It was a ludicrous ambition for someone who was a foot shorter than me and of chunkier build. I could only think that Shohei was talking metaphorically and his youngest son went on to confirm this.

'My father like fighting spirit. You play Samurai golf. Like warrior. You go for kill.'

In his halting English, he was admiring a facet of my play which has aroused most criticism in my own country. It was true that I had a devil-may-care pugnacity that had won me victories I would not otherwise have come close to achieving, but it had also lost me a number of tournaments and incurred a lot of penalty points in the golfing press. I was no Samurai there. Kinder commentators used words like 'wayward', 'erratic' and 'volatile'. More abusive sections of my fan club started with 'suicidal' and worked downwards. I still could not bring myself to like Fumio Ogino, not least because he seemed to have been manufactured to specification on some golfing assembly line, but I was nevertheless flattered to be one of his early prototypes. It explained why his father had been so keen to entice me to Japan.

Shohei himself came up and his son fell silent.

'Come with me, Alan,' he said firmly. 'We must find somewhere to talk in peace.'

'Lead the way.'

'You will excuse us, Fumio.'

The young golfer gave a token bow as did several other people as Shohei left the room like a departing shogun. I wondered which of the three sons would now use his father's absence to enjoy the opportunity to lord it over the guests. Shohei took me down a long corridor to the rear of the house, then he opened a door and led me into what was obviously his study. It was a big room with the desk as its focal point and an impressive array of electronic marvels from the Ogino factories. Offsetting the technological feel was a three-piece suite in real leather and a black ivory coffee table. Two walls were given over to bookshelves and I noticed the number of golf titles imported from the West. Photographs of the family abounded but it was Fumiko's golfing career that gained most pictorial attention. He was everywhere.

'Do you smoke?' asked my host.

'No, thanks.'

'May I?'

'Of course, Mr Ogino.'

'I always slip into my study around this time,' he said with a sly smile. 'My wife hates me to smoke. She has given me this plastic filter to use but its taste is unbearable. I come in here to have a cigar in comfort.'

'Puff away,' I invited.

'You like my trophies?' he asked, indicating the display on the mantelpiece. 'I have been very lucky.'

His modesty was feigned. Only immense hard work and managerial brilliance could have won him the galaxy of prestigious business awards that stood on the mantelpiece. I could only read the citations that were in English but it was clear from the size and profusion of the objects—not to mention the framed certificates behind them—that Shohei Ogino was an exceptional man and he had brought me into his study primarily to emphasise that fact. He wanted me to feel the full weight of his importance.

Pride of place in the collection, however, did not go to a business award at all. It went to a large silver object that was quite self-explanatory. A miniature green was set in front of a replica of Mount Fuji. Hunched over his ball, a tiny golfer was about to putt. The flagstick stood straight and true in the hole. Fluttering in the imaginary wind was the distinctive red sun on a white background.

'Fumio's first big success,' said the proud father as he noted my curiosity. 'Take a closer look.'

'Thank you.' I picked it up. 'What was the event?'

'It was the work of many tournaments, Alan. That is the trophy for the Japanese Amateur Golfer of the Year.'

As I examined it with interest, Shohei went behind his desk and reached for the large wooden cigar box that stood on the shelf beside it. I was some fifteen feet or more away from him, half-turned towards the mantelpiece. Though I was staring at the flagstick, I saw him—out of the corner of my eye—open the cigar box. It was the last time he would ever do that. The explosion was deafening. It split the box into a million splinters and hurled me sideways against the wall. My head took the impact and I dropped like a stone to the carpet, instinctively turning into the room as I did so. My brain was on fire and every ounce of my energy had gone. Searing pain went through my right hand.

In the second of consciousness that remained, I saw Shohei Ogino slumped across his desk with his face ripped off by the blast. The image pursued me into oblivion.

◇◇◇

When I finally opened my eyes on a new world, I saw a round light fixture on a white ceiling. It was moving about at first but it eventually decided to stay up and came into focus. I narrowed my lids against the glare and tried to move my head. It felt heavy and rather tender and I soon became aware of the bandaging that encircled it. I was lying on my back in a bed that had crisp white linen sheets. When I tried to flex my muscles, I found resistance and so I acted with extreme care. Taking one limb at a time, I began my examination with some gentle stretching and twisting. There was pain but not the sudden stab of any break-age. My attempt to sit up, however, was doomed from the start. Someone cut intricate patterns down my side with the blade of a Stanley knife and I became aware of the extensive bandaging around my body. I was alive but wounded. A slow survey of the room through smarting eyes told me that I was in hospital.

A door clicked, footsteps approached and a nurse leaned over me with brisk concern. When I managed a twitch of my lips by way of a smile, she hurried out and came back almost immediately with a white-coated doctor. He bent over me and spoke quietly in Japanese. I gave him a grunt of acknowledgement then faded back into the twilight world for what seemed like another century or two. My second coming was more positive. The light fixture was firmly in place and its beams no longer attacked the eyes so violently. My nurse was on hand to signal my return and the soft-voiced doctor was soon carrying out another inspection. When they got a series of grunts out of me, they were sufficiently encouraged to lift me gently up into a sitting position. Thick pillows softened the stinging sensation down my back and side.

Something was poured into a beaker then held to my lips by the nurse. Sweet and cool, it did wonders for my voice and I was able to croak my thanks. As my mind began to clear, I had my first fleeting memory of the incident that had put me into the hospital and it made me wince. It was minutes before I dared concentrate hard enough to summon up once more the hideous image of my host in a pool of his own blood. Another drink soothed me and I produced a coherent sentence for the first time.

'Am I going to pull through?'

Though no linguist, the doctor understood what I was asking and gave me the thumbs-up sign. After a few more minutes of gauging my progress, he dispatched the nurse with a muttered command and her heels clacked on the tiled floor. A face that I actually recognised then appeared beside me.

'Remember me?' he said.

'Of course.'

'Who am I?'

'Mr Ushiba.'

'Very good.'

He gave a muffled chuckle then turned to speak to the doctor in Japanese. I was pleased to see Akio Ushiba again because he had been so affable at the clubhouse on my first visit there but I could not understand why he was visiting me in hospital. I then recalled his saying that he worked occasionally for Shohei Ogino and I deduced that he must be here to represent the bereaved family at this harrowing time. In the circumstances, I could hardly expect one of the three sons—still less the wife or daughter—to roll up with a bunch of grapes and a few magazines for me. Akio Ushiba was a most acceptable envoy. He was friendly, cheerful and knew how to get on to my wavelength.

The nurse brought him a chair and he sat beside me.

'How do you feel?' he said.

'A bit delicate.'

'You were very fortunate, Alan.'

I shuddered. '*This* is being fortunate?'

'Severe concussion and many superficial flesh wounds but nothing is broken. They found no internal injuries. You should be out of bed in a couple of days.'

'I want to stay here for a couple of *months*.'

He chuckled again but there was no real humour in it. The situation which had brought us together again was too tragic to be addressed with laughter. Akio Ushiba leaned in closer so that his flabby jowls hung down.

'What happened?' he said.

'You tell me.'

'Think.'

'There was a big bang and that was that.'

'Is that all you remember?'

'No.'

'What else, then?'

'It's…very painful.'

'Take it slowly. No rush.'

I tried to compose my thoughts but there were strange gaps in the sequence. The key moments were clear enough but the linking action and dialogue had vanished. Ushiba was very patient. He put no pressure on me at all. When he saw my confusion, he prompted me with easy gentleness.

'You were talking to Fumio…'

'That's right,' I said.

'Then his father took you out of the room and along to his study.' A wistful smile. 'I daresay it was to smoke one of those dreadful cigars of his. Masako cannot bear them so her husband has to sneak off and have one in private.' He paused and gave me time to catch him up. 'Did he offer you a cigar, Alan?'

'He must have done.'

'What did you say?'

'I must have refused. I don't smoke at all.'

'Where were you standing?'

'In front of the mantelpiece.'

'Why?'

'I don't know.'

'Where you looking at something?'

'Maybe.'

'Holding it in your hand?'

'Holding what?'

'Think hard.'

'It's not there any more.'

'Think what was on the mantelpiece.'

'On it?'

'Shohei's trophies.'

'I vaguely remember…'

'One in particular.'

'It was a long time ago, Mr Ushiba.'

'Something to do with golf?'

'Who knows?'

'A trophy belonging to Fumio?'

Memory came back and I felt a sharp pain in my right hand. I twitched it involuntarily and Ushiba steadied my arm. When I glanced down, my right palm was covered with a little tramline of stitches. I tried to put everything in the correct order. Cigar box. Explosion. Pain. Collapse. The faceless Shohei. Unconsciousness. Where did my hand fit in?'

'Let's go back to this trophy,' said Ushiba.

'Why is it so important?'

'It gashed your hand.'

I saw it at last. 'The flagstick!'

'Yes, the flagstick, my friend. You must have grasped it tight then fallen on your hand.' He shook his head. 'I do not want to look for symbols here but you must know the truth. Your injury was caused by Mount Fuji.'

'It came to a sharp point. I remember now. It was capped with snow.'

'You covered it with blood. To the Japanese people, the mountain is sacred. It hurt you but it also gave you its blessing. You were saved, Alan.'

'Unlike Shohei...'

'Unlike my dear, dear friend.'

I blotted out the gruesome picture that now came into my mind and Ushiba backed off at once, talking instead about the other guests at the party. Nobody else was injured by the blast but several people were being treated for shock and a few of the women—Masako Ogino among them—were being detained in hospital. He brought warm regards from Clive Phelps who was out in the waiting room at that moment. Chiyo Takumi and Hideo Nakane were both with him. I was touched. Stuck in a hospital bed thousands of miles away from home, I could yet count on four sympathetic visitors.

One of them, Akio Ushiba, resumed his questioning.

'What was the last thing you saw, Alan?'

'Mr Ogino...'

'What was he doing?'

'Lying dead across the desk.'

'Before that. Before the explosion.'

'He opened the cigar box...'

Ushiba sat back in his chair with satisfaction then he took me through it all again, reviving my memories and searching for new details, rebuilding the last few minutes of the life of Shohei Ogino with the dedication of a man trying to piece together the shattered cigar box. Only when I began to tire noticeably did he give up and motion in the nurse. She gave me a fresh sip from the beaker then adjusted my pillows for comfort. My visitor stood up and thanked me for my help, promising to come again in due course.

'It was kind of you to find the time,' I said.

'This incident has distressed me a great deal.'

'Who could have done such a thing?'

'He will be tracked down, Alan.'

'It was cold-blooded murder.'

'The criminal will be made to pay.' He reached out a hand to pat me gingerly on the arm. 'Take care.'

'I will. Goodbye, Mr Ushiba.'

'Goodbye, Alan…Oh, and one thing you ought to know.'

'Yes?'

'It is Superintendent Ushiba.'

I reeled from a second explosion. 'A *policeman?*'

'This is my case. You will see a lot of me.'

◇◇◇

The untimely death of Shohei Ogino hit the front pages of the newspapers with the force of a cyclone. Among the civilised countries of the world, Japan was far and away the safest to live in. The streets of Tokyo were largely free of crime and its citizens could travel about by day or night with relative impunity. It could not just be explained by the general passivity of the population and the high degree of civil obedience. There was also a tacit acceptance of the fact that crime simply did not pay and there was a large and efficient police force to reinforce that dictum. Local ward administrative offices recorded the whereabouts of everyone in Tokyo so malefactors were usually traced at some speed. Police-boxes were sprinkled everywhere as a visual warning and as bases from which the law could be enforced in any locality without delay.

Murders were uncommon. Shocking deaths of the kind that Shohei Ogino had suffered in the privacy of his own home were virtually unknown. As a rule, only a gangland vendetta could produce such a sensational murder. The whole nation was stunned when it learned that a prominent and respected businessman had been blown to pieces by some kind of explosive device. Photographs of the deceased and shots of the damaged house accompanied the stark headlines. Almost as an afterthought, the occasional small picture of Alan Saxton was included but it was not important to the hushed readership. I was a *gaijin*, an outsider, an alien. And I had survived. Real concern was focused on the dead man and on his distraught family. Angry editorials urged the police to solve the outrageous crime as soon as possible.

Hideo Nakane rammed home the point. He sat beside my hospital bed with a sheaf of newspapers and translated the more lurid accounts for me. Details of my own part in the saga had been relayed to reporters by the police who felt that I was not yet strong enough to face the inevitable press interrogation. Superintendent Akio Ushiba had posted two men outside my room to protect me. It was one of the few times in my life when I have been grateful to a policeman.

Hideo threw another paper aside in irritation.

'They will start a panic at this rate,' he said.

'Sensationalism?'

'Crime reporters getting things out of proportion.'

'Why are they doing that?'

'The power of the Ogino name.' He shook his head sadly. 'Tokyo usually has only a few murders every month. That is amazing in a city with twelve million people. I mean, I have lived in London and in New York so I know what a real crime wave is like. Newspapers should be there to reassure and not to frighten. They make me sick sometimes.'

It was my second day in hospital and my recovery was well under way. Much of the pain had eased off and the extensive bruising I'd suffered during my fall was slowly changing from a raw purple to a defeatist yellow. I'd still not had the courage to look at myself in the mirror yet but I was thinking and talking with my old clarity. Like everyone else in Tokyo—and with more just cause—I was desperate to know who had executed the murder of Shohei Ogino.

'Did he have many enemies, Hideo?'

'Powerful men can never be wholly popular.'

'Any serious business rivals?'

'Several,' he said, 'but they would not kill him simply because his annual profits are much higher than their own. Our businessmen murder each other in sudden takeovers and boardroom conspiracies. They would never resort to a bomb.'

'Who does that leave?' I asked.

'Some madman with a grudge against him.'

'Would such a person have access to the house?'

'No,' he agreed, 'and he would certainly not be aware of Shohei's fondness for a sly cigar.'

'That narrows the field considerably, then. We have to look at close colleagues within his own corporation.'

'The field may be narrower still, Alan.'

'What do you mean?'

'The family itself.'

'But that's impossible!'

'Is it?'

'Who would stand to gain from his death?'

'His three sons for a start,' he said. 'Within a matter of hours, Takeshi took over as if his whole life had been a preparation for this moment. He is proving himself the strong man in a crisis situation. I am not saying that he is the murderer but he will definitely reap the major benefit.'

'What about Yasayuki and Fumio?'

'They will both prosper from it in the long run.'

'I refuse to believe they were involved.'

'Only time will tell.'

'They respected Shohei so much.'

'Our code of behaviour can sometimes be irksome.'

'No,' I decided. 'I still don't think that any of them would actually kill their father.'

'Haven't you ever wanted to kill yours?'

The rejoinder was too close for comfort and I shook my head to dismiss the grim countenance of Inspector Tom Saxon that suddenly popped up in my mind. With all its many drawbacks, Tokyo was still a more pleasant place to be than Leicester. Home had been a daily bomb-blast to me.

We were still debating the possibilities when Chiyo Takumi joined us. Her brave smile did not hide the profound shock from which she was still suffering. Like everyone else who had been at the fateful party, she would bear psychological wounds for the rest of her life.

Chiyo gave me a soft kiss on the cheek and asked how I was feeling. When formalities had been completed, she sat on the chair which Hideo had courteously vacated for her. I was sorry for them both. They had been hired to work on a golf video that had filled them both with enthusiasm but the project had, literally, gone up in smoke. Preoccupied with what had happened to me, I'd had no time to consult my own disappointment but I had sensed theirs and that of Clive Phelps. All three had been made cruelly redundant.

There was a complete surprise in store for me.

'I've been talking to Takeshi,' said Chiyo.

'How is he?' I asked.

'Deeply hurt, of course, but he has a strong nerve. He rang me at my hotel this morning with the news.'

'What news?' said Hideo.

'The project will be completed.'

'Our video?' I gasped.

'It meant so much to Shohei,' she explained. 'He loved the game with all his heart. Takeshi believes his father would have wanted us to go on. He is now insisting on it. We must make it as an act of affirmation.'

'I can understand that,' murmured Hideo.

Chiyo smiled hopefully. 'It's up to you, Alan. I am keen to press on and finish the project but I will not blame you if you wish to pull out. Tokyo has not been very hospitable to you so far.' She touched my arm. 'What do you say?'

'Count me in.'

'Thank you!' she said as tears welled up.

'I came here to do a job and I'll do it,' I said. 'When I'm fit enough to hold a club again. Besides, I have another reason for staying in Tokyo.'

'What's that?' said Hideo.

'I'm going to find the bastard who planted that bomb.'

Chapter Six

After another night in hospital, I was well enough to be divested of some of my bandaging and discharged. I felt very stiff and my lacerations still smarted but I was able to walk without too much difficulty. Since the stitches were due to be removed from my hand the next day, I had the distinct feeling that I was on the mend. The luxurious facilities of the Imperial Hotel were never more welcome and I was able to succumb willingly to their seductive charms as I tried to recharge the batteries. Clive Phelps had urged me to fly the flag. Though it had almost been reduced to half-mast in Shohei Ogino's study, it was still fluttering bravely above my instructional video. There was life after death.

The police investigation had cracked into top gear with Superintendent Akio Ushiba at the driving wheel. An incident room had been set up and a veritable army of detectives had been assigned to it. Forensic experts had combed through the wreckage at the home itself to find clues as to the nature and origin of the explosive device. Intensive house-to-house questioning was instituted in the surrounding area in case anyone had seen anything at all suspicious going on near the property in question, and known bomb-makers with criminal records were rounded up for routine interrogation. Lying on a cold table at the pathology lab, the mutilated body of Shohei Ogino provided what help he could to the probing medicos who clustered around him. An appalling mess had been created in the middle of Tokyo. The onus was on the police to clean it up as soon as possible.

Progress was tediously slow. As the shock of the murder wore off, it was replaced by indignation that no arrests had as yet been made. In a city where the police force prided itself on its eternal vigilance, there was growing fear that here was a heinous crime committed right under their noses by someone too guileful to be caught. At the lower end of the newspaper market, this fear was exploited by banner headlines asking if the miscreant would strike again? Was he still at large in Tokyo? Who was next on his death list? Cartoons added to the general hysteria.

I was very grateful to the hotel management for my free daily copy of *The Japan Times*, an English-language newspaper that kept me abreast of latest developments in a sane and well-informed way. According to the paper—All The News Without Fear or Favour—the death of Shohei Ogino had been a devastating blow to the thousands of employees in his factories and office blocks but they had quickly rallied behind the senior vice-president of the corporation, Takeshi Ogino, the eldest son of the deceased. The Japanese machine might miss a few beats but it would never actually stop. The king was dead. Long live the king.

Another newspaper which I read at the hotel was *The Bangkok Times*. Viewing the case from a more distant perspective, it yielded some interesting comments about the nature of Japanese business life and its obituary of the dead man was much more perfunctory than the fulsome praise showered upon him by the media in his own country. *The Bangkok Times* also furnished me with a vital reminder.

'Sam?'

'Yes. Who is this?'

'Alan Saxon.'

'Alan! How *are* you?'

'I'm calling from Japan.'

'We've heard the news about Ogino.'

'It's organised chaos at this end.'

'What about *you*, Alan? How badly were you hurt?'

Sam Limsong sounded genuinely upset on my behalf when I telephoned him so I gave him the latest medical bulletin and assured him that I would be back on a golf course in a couple of days. When I asked him for his reaction to the murder, however, his tone hardened into indifference.

'No comment,' he said.

'But you *knew* him, Sam.'

'I know lots of people.'

'How many get blown to pieces by an explosive device?'

'I never liked Shohei Ogino.'

'Why not?'

'It's personal.'

'And highly relevant at this moment.'

'Back off, Alan.'

'I need help here.'

'Then you've come to the wrong place,' he said. 'Sorry. If you want help or sympathy, you'll have to go somewhere else. I'm not going to say respectful things about that old tyrant simply because he's been murdered. Why be dishonest about it? I'm *glad* that he's dead.'

'There must be a reason for that.'

'Maybe.'

'Come on, Sam,' I urged. 'For heaven's sake, I was damn near killed myself! This matters to me! I need every scrap of assistance that I can get.'

'Not from me, Alan.'

'Was it something to do with Fumio?'

'I have to go, I'm afraid…'

'He beat you in a play-off recently, didn't he?'

'Thanks for calling.'

'Or was it a personality clash between you and Shohei?'

'Goodbye, Alan.'

'Don't hang up on me.'

'I've nothing more to add.'

'Go away and think about it,' I suggested. 'Let me ring you again when you've had time to mull it over.'

'No point.'

'Sam, I thought we were friends!'

'We are.'

'Then why the stonewalling?'

A hesitant pause was followed by a gabble. 'I really have to be off, Alan. Don't bother to ring again because I'm flying back to the States in a day or two. Shohei Ogino is dead but I didn't kill him. I was here in Bangkok when it happened. That lets me out.'

He put down the receiver before I could even speak.

The shadows on the grass lengthened considerably.

◇◇◇

The funeral of Shohei Ogino was held on the next day. A body which has suffered multiple indignities was at last released to the family so that it could be cremated according to Buddhist rite. I went to the ceremony with deep misgivings and they were not stilled by what I witnessed. As soon as I saw the coffin, I was reminded strongly of the last moment of its occupant's life and my wounds momentarily reopened. I also felt the pull of guilt for the first time, asking myself if I was not in some way indirectly responsible for the tragedy. It was only because I had fallen foul of Ogino with a chance remark that I was invited into his private sanctum at all. Some attempt at reconciliation was evidently about to be made and it was this—rather than any uncontrollable urge for a cigar—which had taken him into the danger zone.

Conducted by a Buddhist priest, the ceremony was short and very moving. Funerals in Japan are highly expensive and many families cannot easily bear the cost themselves but that was not the case here. Unlike many of his employees who had passed away, Shohei Ogino did not have to rely on any contribution from his boss or his colleagues. In death as in life, he paid his own way. Hideo Nakane was again a tower of strength, giving me a muted commentary throughout the funeral and translating some of the priestly incantations. When fire began to consume the last remains of the deceased, Hideo broke off to stand in respectful silence along with the other mourners.

The irony of it all seemed brutal. A man who had reached into a box for a cigar was himself now going up in smoke. The partial cremation effected by an explosive device was being completed in a controlled and proper way. His ashes would be buried in the cemetery in a plot marked by an elaborate gravestone. My own father shouldered his way into my mind. What were his wishes for his funeral? Did he wish to be buried or cremated? Had he confided in Dorothy something he could not communicate to his son? It had been an unhappy week for me, beginning with one funeral in Leicester and ending with another in Tokyo. In both cases, Tom Saxon bulked large. I could not evade him.

Contemplation of my own father led me on to reflections about the sons of Shohei Ogino. All three were in stone-faced attendance, watching the wisps of smoke climb up into the blue sky as the shaven-headed priest spoke the ritual prayers. Takeshi had grown visibly in power and status since I had last seen him, supporting his weeping mother and staring ahead of him with an expression of determined grief. Yasayuki was standing beside his sister, Mitsu, holding her by the elbow as she swayed slightly, then closing his eyes in gratitude when the ordeal was finally over. Fumio Ogino was a glowering presence, his flashy good looks at variance with the prevailing solemnity. The three brothers should have been united by the disaster but they had never looked so separate from each other as at that moment in time.

Another figure caught my attention. Akio Ushiba was mingling with the mourners, paying his own last respects to a friend while remaining on duty. I wondered how many of his detectives had infiltrated the crowd in order to keep watch over the ceremony. A callous murderer might well take some pleasure in the last rites of his victim but he did not seem to have turned up on this occasion. Ushiba knew how to become invisible and remain alert.

As we began to disperse, I felt a tug at my sleeve and saw that Chiyo Takumi was beside me, her face pallid and her eyes red from weeping. I slipped an arm around her and took her aside for a few words.

'Are you okay?' I said.

'I'm fine now.'

'It was pretty harrowing.'

'I hate funerals.'

'It's over now, Chiyo.'

'If only it was,' she said. 'I think it's going to hang around our necks for a long time. Shohei may have gone in body but he will still be here in other ways.'

'Yes,' I noted. 'He's been reincarnated as his eldest son. Takeshi is already starting to look like Shohei II.'

'Take me out of here, Alan.'

'We'll find a taxi.'

'I'm sorry to be such a drag.'

'You're nothing of the kind, Chiyo.'

I guided her down to the road but she stopped abruptly.

'Alan…'

'Yes.'

'We've *got* to finish that video,' she insisted.

'And we will.'

'For his sake. We owe it to Shohei.'

'I go along with that.'

'Thank you.'

Chiyo began talking about the project again to cheer herself up and it had evidently taken on an almost missionary quality for her. I was still trying to make sense of the funeral rites that I had just witnessed. While she was looking to the future, I was still reviewing something in the immediate past—the Ogino family video in which I had just participated. It was supremely instructional.

◇◇◇

Next morning found me restored enough to be able to face breakfast with Clive Phelps in my room. He was still in a sombre mood. The explosion at the Ogino home had made a deep impression on him and robbed him temporarily of his freewheeling lust. Gone were the endless fantasies and the crude innuendoes. He had not mentioned the live sex shows in Roppongi for days, he had left the female members of the hotel staff entirely unmolested and he had even abandoned his reflex pursuit of Chiyo. But the most telling sign of all was the fact that he had rung his wife no less than four times in a row as if touching his emotional base just to make sure that it was there. This was not the Jekyll and Hyde character that I'd known and loved for so long, the happy family man who turned into a seasoned voluptuary the moment he was out on his latest assignment. Clive had been sobered. As he munched his warm croissant, he made no wistful references to a conquest of his from Argentina.

'I spoke to Judith again last night,' he volunteered.

'She'll wonder what's wrong with you.'

'I had to put her mind at rest.'

'You've never bothered about your wife before, Clive.'

'Of course I have,' he said testily, brushing some crumbs off his lap. 'I think about her every day. Almost. Golf writers are like sailors. We may voyage around the world but we need a fixed point from which to navigate. And that's what Judith is to me.' He gulped down the last of the croissant. 'What about Rosemary?'

'Eh?' I was startled.

'You've contacted her, surely?'

'I certainly haven't.'

'But you must, Saxon,' he said. 'Where's your sense of consideration. This story has been picked up in all the papers back home, especially mine. DEATH IN TOKYO. OUR GOLF CORRESPONDENT ESCAPES THE INFERNO. Oh, and they had a mention of you, of course. A mug-shot in most papers. Poor old Rosemary must have seen her ex-husband leering up at her over the breakfast table. She'll be *worried*, man.'

'Yes. Afraid that I might survive.'

'Even Rosemary is not that hard-hearted.'

'Don't you believe it,' I said. 'If she ever donates her heart after death, they'll need a stonemason to chisel it out. Yes, and he'll find my name already engraved on it. *Hiciacet* Alan Saxon. R.I.P.'

'You rushed too quickly into divorce, old son,' he said sagely. 'Rosemary was a quality woman. Nothing like long legs and a touch of real class. Give me an English rose any day of the week. Rosemary was a real thoroughbred.'

'With the instincts of a Rottweiler.'

'Your father liked her.'

'That was the crippling blow.'

'What about Lynette?' he asked, using a paper napkin to dab at a coffee-stained moustache. 'Have you contacted her?'

'Days ago. Rang her at school to reassure her that I was still in one piece. She was thrilled. Then she began complaining that *I* was the one who had all the adventures while she's stuck at Benenden having Double Maths with Miss Pomeroy. Adventures! What's adventurous about being in the middle of a bomb-blast!'

'Let's keep off the subject,' he begged.

'We can't,' I said. 'I need a spot of help.'

'Oh God! How many times have I heard that before?'

'You're a trained news-gatherer, Clive.'

'I'm an alcoholic golf writer.'

'The two are not mutually exclusive. You know how to dig around for gossip. Get your spade out and find out all you can about Shohei Ogino.'

'Read the obituaries in the papers.'

'They only tell us about the public man. I want to know what he was really like and how well those sons of his got on with him. I had strange vibrations in that house.'

'You were standing too close to Mitsu.'

'Check her out as well,' I ordered. 'She doesn't fit into the family album somehow. Find out why.'

'Hideo is the man for this job.'

'I've pumped him as much as I dare.'

'But he has contacts. He speaks the bloody lingo.'

'That's his problem. For all his westernisation, he's still Japanese at heart. And we're both *gaijins*. There's a limit to what Hideo will confide.'

'Why do I always get the shitty end of the stick?'

'There's no answer to that, Clive.'

He found several—all of them obscene—but I beat him off and cowed him into a snarling resignation. He was still shaken by the explosion but I had suffered far more physical damage and that enabled me to pull rank. The project, after all, had been his brainchild and he felt responsible for having brought me all that way and exposed me to such danger. I sent him off with a list of things that I needed to know then finished my breakfast. I was about to draw a bath when there was a tap on the door. Expecting it to be Clive again, I threw it wide open and was astonished to see two grisly figures standing there. One was a brawny man with a crew cut who looked like a nightclub bouncer and the other was Fumio Ogino.

It was the young golfer who pushed me back into the room and stepped in after me with his colleague. Crew Cut closed the door behind him and leaned against it like a heavy in a gangster film. His obviousness did not detract from his very real menace. Fumio scowled at me.

'You go, I think,' he snapped.

'Where?'

'Home. You leave Japan.'

'But we haven't finished the video yet.'

'Forget. Just go at once.'

'Takeshi wouldn't like that.'

'I tell you what to do.'

'Sorry, Fumio. We take our orders from the boss.'

'No listen to Takeshi. *Me* the golfer.'

'Your brother is the one who makes the decisions now.'

'I do!'

'Why not take it up with him?'

'You leave my country. Not wanted.'

'I'm sorry you feel that way.'

'My father die because of you.'

'Now wait a minute…'

'He go into room with Alan Saxon. Not come out alive.'

'You can hardly blame that on me.'

'Book flight! No more warnings!'

I reasoned with him at length but it was all in vain. Fumio Ogino identified me as the indirect cause of his father's death. Now that the funeral was over, he was able to throw his weight around a bit more and he had brought some muscle to back him up. Crew Cut had the sort of battered features that have been through scores of fist-fights and I had the feeling that his opponents usually came off worst. In my weakened state, I did not feel up to any physical confrontation and so I backed away from further argument. Taking my silence as consent, Fumio went to the door that was now opened by his companion.

'We no need you teach us how to play golf.'

'Cheerio,' I encouraged.

'Don't make us come back.'

He went out. After a final glare, Crew Cut joined him.

Shohei Ogino's funeral had been less than twenty-four hours ago and yet his younger son was already flexing his muscles. It was a bad omen. I spied little comfort from the other two brothers. They had their power agendas as well.

I could be crushed between all three of them.

◇◇◇

Superintendent Akio Ushiba was issuing orders to two of his men when I was conducted into the office. He had requested my presence at the police station and sent a squad car to fetch me. There was moderate excitement in being able to speed through a city whose traffic was still heavy in the late morning. Ushiba dismissed his detectives and beamed in welcome at me, following in up with a warm handshake.

'You look like a new man, Alan,' he said.

'I feel much better.'

'Good, good.'

'You said on the phone you had something to show me.'

'Do not rush me, my friend. Everyone is doing that.' He pointed to the newspapers on his desk. 'They are hounding me to make an arrest. They expect instant detection. But it is not as easy as that, as you well know.' The old chuckle was back again. 'Being the son of a policeman.'

'It's something I try to forget, Superintendent.'

'I hope you are not ashamed of it.'

'Just fatigued.'

He nodded and became serious. 'I saw you at the funeral yesterday. It was a very sad occasion. Shohei was such an interesting man if you got close to him. I will miss him.'

'Do you have any leads?'

'You are rushing me again, Alan,' he said with mock reproach. 'Police work is slow and methodical. We have to sift all the evidence before we make a final judgement.'

'But you must have theories, Superintendent.'

'Dozens of them.'

'Such as?'

'Let us stick to facts for the moment, shall we?' He moved towards a door. 'There is someone else here as well. Let us go through and meet him.'

He took me into the adjoining room which was much larger and filled with long trestle tables arranged in parallel lines. Each table was covered with a series of small objects and fragments, all neatly imprisoned in plastic bags and docketed. Standing between the rows of tables so that he could move from one line to another was Yasayuki Ogino, poring over the collection with the intensity of a scientist on the brink of an important discovery. He did not look up until he heard the door shut behind us.

'Good morning,' he said.

'Hello,' I replied, exchanging a handshake.

'We are very sorry this has happened to you.'

'Forget me, Yasayuki. Your father is more important.'

'You suffered as well. In our home.'

'Alan is made of strong stuff,' said Ushiba, giving me a pat of approval on the shoulder. 'English teak.'

'I felt more like balsa wood at the time.'

'Quite so.' The Superintendent flicked a hand at the tables. 'This is the debris from the study. Hours of careful work by dozens of men have gone into the display but it has given us one vital piece of information.'

'What's that?'

'How the bomb was planted.'

'That is what puzzled me,' admitted Yasayuki, scratching his forehead. 'How could anyone take my father's cigar box away from his study for long enough?'

'It was a very sophisticated device,' added Ushiba. 'Semtex explosive. A delicate trigger mechanism. It would've taken some time to secure all the wiring.'

'Then how was it done?' I asked.

'Like this.'

He handed me a plastic bag that was filled with a large pile of loose shavings. I guessed at once that they were the fragments of the cigar box which had blown up in Shohei Ogion's face. Ushiba gave me another plastic bag. The pieces of wood were much bigger this time and I could guess why.

'There were *two* cigar boxes,' I said.

'Well done,' congratulated the Superintendent. 'The original one never left the study. It was in the replica that the device was fitted. The second box then replaced the first which was hidden behind the curtain where it had some protection from the blast.' He pointed to each plastic bag in turn. 'Replica box with bomb. Real box with cigars.'

'But who put it in the study?' asked Yasayuki.

'We will find him, whoever he is,' said Ushiba. 'Or whoever *they* are. This is not the work of one man.'

Yasayuki switched to Japanese to question the other more closely and, I guessed, to prevent me from eavesdropping on their conversation. Though the words were beyond me, their body language was eloquent. Like his elder brother, Yasayuki had taken on a more positive character in the wake of his father's death and he both expected and got a measure of deference from the Superintendent. Closer acquaintance with the middle of three sons confirmed Hideo's assessment. Yasayuki Ogino was the most interesting and intelligent of all of them and he lacked nothing in ambition.

Ushiba showed him a few more items on the table then they shook hands. Yasayuki gave me a formal smile and a nod before slipping out of the room to leave us alone.

'He has been most helpful,' said Ushiba.

'In what way?'

'Identifying all this, for a start. And letting me into some of the secrets of the Ogion factory. Yasayuki is the family genius. He is—what's the English word…?'

'Boffin?'

'Yes.' He chuckled again. 'He is their boffin.'

'And what area was he working on?'

'That is confidential, I'm afraid.'

'I see.'

He continued quickly. 'But the other thing he was able to do was to give one of my theories some support. This may sound a little odd at first but…'

'Go on.'

'Shohei may not have been the intended victim.'

'Who else?'

'Takeshi. It seems that he was fond of cigars as well. His father allowed him to help himself from the box.' He held his palms open and shrugged. 'Who was supposed to trigger that explosion? Father or son?'

'Or both together.'

'Another possibility.'

'If the box was being offered by one to the other, both would have been killed,' I said. 'That's what saved *me*. I was on the other side of the room because I didn't smoke.'

'Filthy habit. Gets you one way or the other.'

He walked down the table and lifted up another bag to wave at me. I recognised the golfing award I'd been holding at the critical moment and noticed that the flagstick was now bent over at an acute angle. Japanese pride had been severely dented. Its national flag was being lowered. Ushiba returned it to the table and pointed a finger at me.

'*Why*, Alan?' he said.

'Mm?'

'Why did Shohei take you into his study?'

'To talk to me.'

'About what?'

'Who knows?'

'We must find out. It could be significant.'

'I don't follow.'

'This was on his desk.'

He handed me a few scraps of shiny paper covered with an illustration and a list of numbers. They were encased in another piece of plastic but I saw at once what they were.

'Parts of a card of the course.'

'An *English* golf course.'

'Which one?'

'Packwood Heath.'

'I know it, Superintendent. It's in Northants.'

'Have you played there?'

'Many years ago but I have fond memories. Good course for the average club golfer. Well-wooded and -bunkered. I think there's a stream that affects play on four or five holes.' I was still bewildered. 'Why should Shohei Ogino be interested in a golf course in England?'

'He was hoping to buy it.'

'*Buy* it?'

'I think that's what he wanted to discuss with you.'

◇◇◇

A working lunch at the Imperial Hotel gave the four of us a chance to pool our ideas. Chiyo Takumi was back to her most vigorous, Hideo Nakane was as quietly positive as ever and Clive Phelps rallied at the notion of getting on with the project that had brought us to Japan in the first place. At the moment, we were in limbo and it was telling on all of us. The sooner we could lose ourselves in our work again, the better it would be.

I was the crucial factor. Though my recovery had been rapid, I would not yet be able to hit all those stylish shots required by the script.

Chiyo had the solution to our problem.

'Scrap our original schedule,' she said confidently. 'We shoot out of sequence instead. Alan may not be up to the fancy stuff yet so we concentrate on his putting.'

'Could you manage that?' Clive asked me.

'Just about,' I said. 'But it's not my putting I'd be worried about. It's my appearance. What about all these tiny cuts down the side of my face?'

'We don't see them,' explained Chiyo. 'With some careful make-up, I'm sure that Keiko can hide most of the blemishes. In any case, the camera will favour your good side.'

Clive grinned. 'He doesn't *have* a good side.'

We all laughed and the show was back on the road again. After the way that it had been stopped in its tracks, we were all immensely relieved and new ideas flowed thick and fast. Chiyo then went off to telephone her camera crew and book their services for the following morning. Hideo gave us a digest of press reaction in the day's papers to the apparent lack of progress in the murder investigation. The serious newspapers were taking a responsible line on the whole thing but there was still a lot of anxiety-mongering at the lower end of the market. Extra police had been drafted in to guard the Ogino household because it was now attracting so much ghoulish interest from visitors.

'You have to feel sorry for the family,' said Clive with a sigh. 'As if they didn't have enough to put up with.'

'They'll pull through,' observed Hideo flatly. 'The Ogino dynasty is very resilient. Look at the way they've coped so far.'

'Bit frightening, really,' I admitted.

'Who will eventually come out on top?' I wondered. 'Takeshi, Yasayuki or Fumio?'

'Yes,' said Clive. 'Rag, Tag or Bobtail?'

'It will be interesting to see,' murmured Hideo.

Chiyo returned and finalised the arrangements for the following day. She and Hideo then left, Clive went off to do some more research on my behalf and I took the opportunity to soak my wounds in a deep foam bath. Work on the video had given us a common purpose again but my mind was still exercised by recent events. My visit to the police station had thrown up fascinating new information but it was the lead I was keeping to myself that most intrigued me. What had caused the bad blood between Sam Limsong and Shohei Ogino? When had the bugging device been planted in my golf bag? And why? All roads led to Bangkok. It was there that a vital link in the chain would be found and I made a mental note to ring my Thai friend again. He knew something that might open up a whole new avenue to us.

I was still speculating what it might be when there was a buzz beside my ear. Wiping a soapy hand on a towel, I lifted the receiver from its wall socket and put it to my ear. The voice I heard was soft, breathy and very frightened.

'Is that Alan Saxon, please?'

'Speaking.'

'Are you on your own?'

'Completely.'

'I have a special favour to ask.'

'Go ahead. I'll do whatever I can for you.'

'Thank you.' A worried pause. 'I must see you soon.'

'Today?'

'If possible.'

'Would you like to come here?'

'No, that is not good. It will have to be somewhere else. Somewhere very discreet.' The tinkling laugh was now an embarrassed titter. 'I'm sorry but there is good reason.'

'I understand.'

'Tonight?'

'Just give me a time and place.'

'Right…'

I memorised the details and assured her that nobody else would know about the meeting. It was strictly between the two of us and it might turn out to be the most illuminating yet with a member of that family. Thanking me profusely, she rang off and left me to ponder a question that was fraught with all kinds of possibilities.

Why had Mitsu Ogino arranged a rendezvous with me?

Chapter Seven

Clive Phelps had extraordinary powers of recovery. Deeply disturbed by the explosion at the Ogino party, he had been frightened into an unaccustomed fidelity for some days now and deprived of all those compulsive urges that afflict him the moment he is out of sight of his wife and family. The miracle could not last and I was sad to be the agent of its demise. Crude envy terminated his unwonted celibacy.

'What's her name, Saxon?' he said accusingly.

'It's a man. A business contact.'

'Don't give me that crap, matey. If you're sloping off alone for an evening in Tokyo, there's only one conceivable explanation. You're chasing pussy.'

'I'm not, Clive.'

'Okay, then. Take me with you.'

'I'm afraid I can't.'

'Why not?'

'Because it's a private matter.'

'Between you and her.'

'Between me and *him*.'

'You can't fool me, Saxon. I can always smell a bonk.' His moustache twitched with curiosity. 'Who is she?'

'Nobody you know.'

'Ah, then it is a woman!'

'Maybe.'

I had to mislead him in order to get him off my back. As soon as I told him that I could not have dinner with him that evening, he jumped to the only conclusion that exists in his lexicon. Jealousy aroused and lust rekindled, Clive was a one-man Spanish Inquisition and I was forced to give him a partial confession in order to be spare further tortures.

'How did you meet her?' he said.

'She's a friend of a friend.'

'Japanese?'

'Very.'

'They're the best, take my word.'

'I will, Clive.'

'They know how to please a man. It's an art-form out here. They work at it. I remember reading this Japanese pillow book once. Astounding! Your average Englishwoman would never do any of that. All you get from her is a Bare Minimum Fuck followed by "Was I all right, darling?" Not these Jappo girls. They go all the way and much further.' He was into full stride now. 'According to the book, Japanese wives are supposed to present their posteriors to their husbands to signal total submission to his will. Just think of all those beautiful Oriental bums winking up at you, Saxon.' He sniggered happily. 'You'd be able to have Rodeo Sex.'

I knew there was a joke coming and I had to let him get it out. When Clive is on a roll, he is unstoppable.

'What's Rodeo Sex?' I cued.

'That's when you take the missus from behind, bonk away for a bit, then say: "Eh, this is great! I do it like this with my girl-friend." Then you try and stay on for ten seconds!' He laughed uproariously. 'I love that gag.'

'Wonder why.'

It was mid-evening and we were sitting in the lounge at the Imperial Hotel. Apart from the break at lunch, Clive had spent the whole day doing some strenuous legwork at my behest and he had every right to expect to be cossetted when he got back. Instead of that, I was ditching him to go out. His research had been thorough because he has privileged access to the freemasonry of the press. Visits to English-language newspapers and magazines had yielded a thick file of cuttings about Shohei Ogino and his family. Off-the-record chats over a drink or two had brought in a wealth of gossip and rumour. Having rushed back to deliver it all, he found me on my way out to what he decided simply had to be an assignation.

'You might have warned me, Saxon,' he complained.

'It came up suddenly.'

'I have that trouble all the time.'

'It was an invitation I couldn't refuse.'

'I feel jilted.'

'Give your wife a ring.'

'Cast aside without compunction.'

'I got a better offer.'

'Two-timing turd!'

'Sorry, Clive.'

'Dark Horse Saxon—that's you!'

'Even a dark horse is entitled to a gallop.'

A wild thought put a lecherous gleam into his eye.

'Maybe she has a friend.'

'I'm it.'

He swore under his breath and walked across to the main entrance with me. I took a first dip into his fact file.

'What's the verdict on Shohei Ogino?'

'Death by cigar box.'

'Was he crooked?'

'Up to every fiddle in the book but he always got away with it. These moguls have to sail close to the wind in order to survive. Shohei took more chances than most but he had friends in high places and a team of smart lawyers watching his arse.'

'What about his sons?'

'They don't like each other.'

'I'd worked that bit out for myself.'

'Takeshi is the supershit, by all accounts. Nobody likes him. One of those power-mad tycoons with ice in his veins. He was held back by his father but now he's had lift off. Takeshi made his mark in hours, let alone days. All round the Ogino empire, knees are knocking like castanets.'

'What's the score with Yasayuki?'

'Those two don't see eye to eye at all,' said Clive as we stepped out into the street. 'What British politicians call a difference of emphasis.'

'In other words, fundamental disagreement.'

'You've got it. Takeshi wants to streamline the company and invest much more abroad. Yasayuki thinks that research should be their priority. He's the Ideas Man in the set-up and came up with some real winners.'

'Which didn't endear him to his elder brother.'

'Exactly.'

'So Takeshi will try to clip his wings.'

'Who's telling this story—me or you?'

'You, of course,' I soothed. 'But we'll have to take a commercial break while I go off for my date with Destiny.'

'Lucky sod!'

'Fortune favours the brave.'

'Bollocks!'

I raised an arm to flag down a taxi and its indicator came blinking towards us. As we strolled to the kerb, I tried to sound as casual as possible.

'Find anything out about the sister?' I said.

'Quite a bit. Mitsu is a real cracker.'

'Anyone can see that.'

'She's the one true human being in the family.'

'Why?'

'Because she stood up to her father.'

'Mitsu told me he'd encouraged her all the way.'

'Family propaganda.'

The door of the taxi had opened electronically and I slid inside. Clive leaned in after me to end his report.

'It's like a temperature gauge.'

'What is?'

'This flipping family. Younger they get, more they warm up. Old Takeshi is freeze-arse cold. Yasayuki is a mild thaw. Fumio is hot and climbing. And Mitsu, I hear— and suspect from personal observation—could be an absolute scorcher.' He slammed my door shut. 'Pity you're not taking *her* out, Saxon. She'd singe it off for you.'

I gave him my inscrutable smile.

◇◇◇

The taxi pulled away from the hotel and drove around the perimeter of the Imperial Palace. Set amid the soaring towers that house the headquarters of the country's major banking and industrial institutions, the palace was for centuries the stronghold of the Tokugawa shoguns before being handed over to the imperial family. Even in its reconstructed state—it was virtually destroyed by fire-bombs in 1945—it is still a powerful symbol of Japan's history and is duly revered. Since the palace is encircled by inner moats and high stone walls, there is very little for the passer-by to see, especially when he is being whisked along at night in a yellow cab, but one feature could not go unnoticed. The Imperial Palace was under heavy armed guard. With the enthronement of Emperor Akihito only weeks away, the police were taking no chances. They had saturated the area with mobiles and with foot patrols.

As we drove past yet another police post, I thought how much my father would enjoy the sight of so many official uniforms. Tokyo would be a home from home to him. His income would be higher, his status greater and his field of operations much wider. More to the point, his crime statistics would be ridiculously lower. Inspector Tom Saxon would love the sense of control and influence that his counterparts seemed to exercise. An event on the scale of an enthronement would give him limitless possibilities with the loud-hailer and the pointing finger. I stopped looking out of the window because my childhood was now flashing past.

We left the spacious feel of Marunouchi and went on through the narrower thoroughfares of Kanda, moving in fits and starts as we hit the mandatory traffic jams. There was more character here, more idea of how the ordinary people of Tokyo lived and worked, more hints of the dark edges around the glittering façade of the economic miracle. The taxi managed a surge over the last mile or so and found the place written on the piece of paper I had given to the driver. Fares are exorbitant in Tokyo and I felt I was buying the vehicle itself as I paid up but there was no alternative. The telephone call from Mitsu Ogino had been a cry of help. You could not put a price on that.

I had been deposited near one of the entrances to Ueno Park, the largest of its kind in the city, and the home of museums and art galleries as well as a library, a festival hall and some famous zoological gardens. Also sited there is the Toshogu Shrine, a five-storey pagoda that dates back over three hundred and fifty years. None of these tourist attractions was open or available to me because I was too busy counting trees. When I reached the twentieth trunk to the left of the gate, I waited as I had been told, wondering yet again why such elaborate precautions were necessary. My watch assured me that I was bang on time but there was no sign of Mitsu. Five minutes went by as I lurked beneath the overhanging branches of a cherry tree, then the car came cruising down the road. Its lights flashed twice before it halted just long enough for me to recognise it as a Honda Accord and to get in. We accelerated away.

Mitsu Ogino was at the driving wheel. She threw me a glance of welcome then kept one eye on the rear-view mirror. This was not the intelligent and assertive young woman I had met at the party. She was now tense, drawn and frightened.

'Thank you for coming,' she began.

'It sounded important.'

'It is.'

'Where are we going?'

'Somewhere quiet.'

She swung the car left and filtered into the line of traffic before making a sudden turn to the right that had several other drivers hanging on their horns in protest. Mitsu ignored the cacophony. She continued to weave in and out of a maze of streets until her mirror was quite clear. Relaxing slightly, she turned down a long neon-lit avenue then picked a side-road that led us into a quiet residential area. Keeping out of the pools of light, she parked near a corner so that she had a choice of exits. The engine died.

'What's the problem?' I said.

'Nothing.'

'Was someone following us?'

'No.'

'Then why are you so jumpy?'

She turned to face me and I was able to see her properly for the first time. A week had aged Mitsu Ogino and put an unbecoming hardness into her eyes. She was dressed in a black coat which buttoned at the neck.

'Good to see you again,' she said.

'Sorry it has to be in such sad circumstances.'

'Yes.'

An uncomfortable pause. 'How are you?' I ventured.

'Not good.'

'This must've been a nightmare for you.'

'Sheer hell.'

'All the media attention can't have helped.'

'They've pestered us like mad.'

'How is your mother taking it?'

'Very badly. She's under sedation at the moment. That's why I was able to slip out.' She forced a smile. 'You must be fed up with our family, Mr Saxon.'

'Alan, please,' I corrected. 'And no, I'm not.'

'We've landed you in so much trouble.'

'I don't see it that way, Mitsu.'

'Anybody else in your position would have run away from Tokyo as soon as possible.'

'I'm the odd man out, remember?'

'A boat-rocker.'

'In this case, I'm trying to steady the craft.'

'You're very brave, Alan.'

'Just foolish.'

'Don't be *too* brave.'

An approaching car made her start slightly and flick her gaze to the wing mirror. She watched the vehicle go past and disappear around the bend before she spoke again.

'I am very sorry about all this,' she said.

'Forget it.'

'On behalf of my family, I apologise.'

'No hard feelings. I'm just glad to be alive.'

'I'm glad, too.' A fugitive smile. 'That's why I rang.' She moistened her lips. 'You have been through enough, Alan. I'd hate anything else to happen to you.'

'What else could?'

Another car interrupted the conversation. She went through the same routine as before, only relaxing when it was out of sight. Mitsu played with the top button of her coat and appraised me with distant concern.

'I had to warn you.'

'About what?'

'Fumio. He's been saying some wild things.'

'That doesn't surprise me.'

'He's always been a bit of a hothead,' she explained. 'Fumio has many fine qualities but he also has a lot of anger inside him. On a golf course, he can control that anger and use it to good effect. At other times...' She clasped her hands tight together. 'He blames you, Alan. Because you were in the study when Father was killed, he thinks that you are somehow responsible. I've tried to tell him how unfair and ridiculous that is but he won't listen. When Fumio gets hold of an idea, he will not let go. It festers away inside him. It makes him dangerous.'

'How dangerous?'

She weighed her words carefully. 'He was the favourite. Takeshi is only an average golfer and Yasayuki doesn't like the game at all but Fumio had tremendous potential. Father spent a lot of time and money in developing that potential and it was finally starting to pay off. Then...' She gave a resigned shrug. 'Fumio was under a lot of pressure. Father wanted results and he pushed him very hard. It was a kind of obsession. Can you understand that?'

'Only too well. I have that obsession myself.'

'But it hasn't warped you, Alan,' she said. 'It hasn't brought out the worst side of your character. That's what it's done to Fumio, you see. The pressure got to him. It's made him ruthless. And violent. When things don't go exactly as he wants them to, he lashes out. People get hurt.'

'Is that what happened to Sam Limsong?'

She drew back sharply as if I'd struck her across the face and a hand came up to her lips. I muttered an apology but she dismissed it with a shake of the head, recovering quickly from her severe discomfort.

'All I'm saying is this, Alan,' she continued. 'Fumio needs to let off steam occasionally. He goes to nightclubs in Roppongi with his "friends". They are not nice people. He's fallen in with a bad crowd.'

I had a feeling I'd met one of them at my hotel. Crew Cut was a bad crowd in himself, a smirking thug who belonged to the world of sleaze and brawl. He was a nocturnal animal who had been brought out of the darkness to act as a frightener. I wondered if Fumio had employed his services against Sam Limsong.

'Why is your brother so hostile towards me?' I said.

'Father's death has upset him deeply.'

'Deranged him, you mean.'

'Yes,' she admitted. 'That is not too strong a word. He has all this anger swirling around inside and he needs to fix it on something. Or on someone.'

'Me.'

'I'm afraid so.'

'Can't you reason with him?'

'I've tried. So has Takeshi. It's hopeless.'

'So Fumio is keeping me in his sights.'

'Very much so. You committed the biggest crime of all.'

'What's that?'

'Being a better golfer.'

A third car awakened her fears and she switched on the ignition. We were soon gliding through another labyrinth of side-streets. Mitsu Ogino had confirmed all that I had suspected from the morning visit by Fumio and Crew Cut. What I had not yet worked out was why she felt impelled to alert me. Was it pure altruism? Hatred of her youngest brother? Or was it some other, as yet undisclosed, reason? I began to probe.

'What about your other brothers?' I asked.

'Takeshi and Yasayuki?'

'How have they responded to the tragedy?'

'They are both deeply shocked.'

'But that hasn't made them turn on me. In fact, I spoke to Yasayuki earlier today. He was as courteous as ever. At the same time…'

'Go on.'

'Well, I can't say that he was exactly dejected.'

'Our family does not seize up when one of its members dies. We keep going. It is what Father would've wanted. Takeshi and Yasayuki respect his wishes. Their main concern is to run the company as efficiently as possible.'

'No decent interval of mourning?'

'They are doing what they feel is necessary.'

'Keeping the wheels turning.'

'It's the Ogino code.'

'Did either of them actually *like* your father?'

'Of course.'

'And you?'

'I was devastated by what happened.'

'Yet the day after his funeral, you're driving around Tokyo with a relative stranger.'

'I only came to warn you.'

'About Fumio?'

'Who else?'

'Your father,' I said. 'And the bits of him that come out in his youngest son. Ambition. Viciousness. And...'

'Stop!' she cried.

The car had come to a sudden halt. Mitsu eyed me warily as if not sure whether to trust or shun me. Inadvertently, I had pressed some button inside her and it made her even more jangled. Her tongue slipped out to moisten her lips again.

'My father was an important man in Tokyo,' she said. 'Everyone respected him. The family worshipped him.'

'But did they love him?'

'In their own way.'

'It doesn't show.'

'You don't understand our culture.'

'I'm beginning to.'

'Father was supreme in our lives.'

'Did *you* love him, Mitsu?'

'Yes!'

'Then why did you defy him?'

'What...?'

'Why did you strike out on your own? Why did you go to America against his wishes? Why did you challenge everything he believed in and assert your independence?'

'I loved him!' she yelled.

But her tears contradicted her tongue. She put the car in motion once again and drove at speed towards Ueno Park. Her face was set in a grimace, her mouth tight, her body tense. Nothing was said until she pulled up near the spot where she had met me earlier on.

'Good night, Alan,' she said.

'Thanks for the ride.'

'I cannot take you back to the hotel.'

'Don't worry.' I opened the door. 'Oh, I know what I meant to ask you.'

'Well?'

'Superintendent Ushiba. He claims that he worked for your father from time to time. In what capacity?'

'Please get out.'

'I ask in the spirit of enquiry.'

'Goodbye.'

'Was Ushiba some sort of…?'

'I've nothing further to say, Alan. Now, *please!*'

I got out of the car and closed the door. It sped away. I'd touched a raw nerve in Mitsu Ogino and it grieved me that she'd left so abruptly but the meeting had been a revelation. It had given me further insight into a strange but intriguing family, and it had firmed up my travel plans.

I might have to go to Bangkok.

◇◇◇

Somjai was not a convincing liar. Her skills lay in her fingers rather than in any manipulation of words. It was a pleasant voice, low and soft, with a strong accent. I was ringing from my room at the Imperial Hotel.

'Hello. Is Sam there, please?' I said.

'Who is this?'

'Alan Saxon.'

There was a pause while she consulted her fiancé. I could almost see him shaking his head and prompting her.

'Er, no. He is not here, Mr Saxon,' she lied.

'Is that Somjai, by any chance?'

'Yes.'

'How do you do? I'm a friend of Sam's.'

'He has mentioned your name.'

'It's vital I get hold of him as soon as possible. Can you give me a number where I might reach him?'

'No, I'm afraid not.'

'But you do know where he is?'

'Well…yes…'

'This is important, Somjai. I need your help.'

Another pause while she took additional advice, then she cleared her throat to pass on the message. I felt sorry for the girl but that did not still my irritation.

'Sam is on the move at the moment,' she said.

'Walking around the room, you mean?'

'I cannot reach him, Mr Saxon.'

'Try sticking your arm out.'

'He is flying back to America tomorrow on the midnight plane. You will not be able to speak to him.'

'Tell him it's about Fumio Ogino.'

'Sorry. That is all I can say.'

'Just put him on for two minutes…'

'Goodbye.'

She hung up on me and left me with no alternative. I grabbed the *Citysource Directory* and found the numbers that I wanted. Japan Airlines, Continental and Qantas were all fully booked but Thai International had a providential cancellation. It was a sign. I followed it recklessly. My already punch-drunk Access Card reeled from the blow of an expensive air ticket but I felt it was worth it. Only direct confrontation with Sam Limsong would produce the truth. Every so often you have to go for the risky long shot.

◇◇◇

A restored and re-activated Clive Phelps was too much to face at the start of another day and so I breakfasted alone in my room. When we left together for the Wada International Country Club, however, I was at his mercy. Our limousine had no sooner pulled away from the kerb than he pounced. A master of the colour action replay himself, he wanted the full details in slow motion.

'How did you make out?' he demanded.

'When?'

'Last night, you sod!'

'Fine. Slept like a log.'

'I'm talking about your date.'

'What date?'

'Look, stop pissing around, will you!' he said testily. 'You sneaked off for a bit of nookie and I have a right to know exactly what it was like. For starters, who was she?'

'A ship that passed in the night.'

He grabbed for the metaphor. 'Did you board her? Scuttle her? Or simply torpedo her below the water line?'

'I just waved.'

'What *with?*'

Clive's raucous laugh set my teeth on edge. He nudged my ribs with come-on-you-can-tell-me familiarity. Nothing is sacred to my friend, no intimacy too great to merit secrecy. When he himself is on the rampage—a fairly regular occurrence—his mind is a non-stop Polaroid camera that never misses a shot. He now insisted on seeing my snaps.

'Spill the beans, Saxon,' he urged. 'What happened?'

'Nothing.'

'Nothing!'

'Nothing at all, Clive.'

'Why not?'

'It was the wrong time of the month.'

He snorted in disgust. 'You fell for *that* old trick.'

'*I* was the one who said it—not her.'

'Are you telling me that you passed up some pussy?'

'Oddly enough, yes.'

'Have you gone stark, staring bonkers!'

'I wasn't in the mood.'

'You're supposed to put *her* in the fucking mood.'

'She wasn't my type.'

'She was a woman, wasn't she? That's type enough.'

'I'm not as undiscriminating as you, Clive.'

'Jesus H Christ!'

'Besides which, I had professional obligations today.'

'That didn't prevent you giving her a quick shag and reporting back the ins and outs of it to Uncle Clive. I've been *waiting* for this, Saxon. Don't let me down now.'

'I behaved like a true gentleman.'

'Screwed her first then thanked her afterwards?'

'Shook hands with her and parted as friends.'

'Are you serious!'

'Some of us operate at a lower voltage than you.'

'I can't believe that I'm hearing this.'

'It's the truth, Clive,' I said. 'Nothing to report.'

'Of all the bloody let-downs!'

'Yes. I suppose I should have taken you, after all.'

'Eh?'

'She did bring a friend, as it happens.'

He pawed at the carpet. 'What!'

'Even more gorgeous than she was. Toyo.'

'Why didn't you bring her back to the hotel for me?'

'Because we'd never have been on the road as early as this, if I had. Toyo had the look of a late riser to me. A lovely body, though. You'd have liked her, Clive…'

I added a few embellishments and he was soon drooling over the fictional possibility that had eluded his grasp. It diverted him from any further questioning. He abused me in ripe language for several minutes and made some very unkind remarks about my manhood but I bore it all in the name of friendship and let the storm blow itself out. I came back with urgent questions of my own.

'Have you ever played at Packwood Heath?' I said.

'In Northants?'

'Yes.'

'I have,' he recalled grimly. 'Not my favourite course. I always manage to lose a couple of balls in that damn stream. Packwood Heath is jinxed. Why do you ask?'

'Shohei Ogino wanted to buy it.'

His interest quickened. 'Did he now?'

'According to Superintendent Ushiba.'

'Old Ogino wouldn't be the first Jap entrepreneur to want a slice of our golfing heritage. The mighty chequebook has already bought Turnberry, not to mention three or four less well-known courses south of the border. Old Thorns is one, down in Hampshire. Then there's Hatfield.'

'Seems so absurd to me.'

'What does?'

'A Tokyo businessman taking an interest in an obscure golf course back in Northamptonshire. I mean, even its best friends wouldn't describe Packwood Heath as exciting.'

'Doesn't matter, old son. Ownership is everything. Ogino would've been making an excellent investment.'

'It's a long way to go for a round of golf.'

'Not if you can't afford to play here,' he said. 'Look at Wada. £1000 per round. Criminal! For the same money, your average Jap tourist can fly to England and have ten days of non-stop golf at somewhere like Packwood Heath. Then there's the thousands of Japs, Koreans and what-have-you who actually live in Britain. They'd think nothing of an hour's drive up to Northampton. Packwood Heath could be a gold mine.'

'What about the existing members?'

'That's what you might call a grey area.'

'They'd be forced out?'

'Adjustments would have to be made.'

'Would Ogino have been allowed to buy?'

'Depends how much he was offering. Course managements have been known to succumb to the power of the yen. The Japs always move in with care. They engage a respectable English land agent to do the sounding out for them. Once interest is established, they come out of the woodwork and start talking numbers.' He clicked his tongue. 'If Shohei Ogino had his beady little eyes on Packwood Heath, you can bet your left testicle that he checked it out first very thoroughly.' A deep sigh escaped him. 'Bit scary, isn't it?'

'What?'

'The Jap invasion. Today, Packwood Heath. Tomorrow, what? Wentworth? Sunningdale? St Andrews even? Makes the old heart go pitter-patter, doesn't it? I mean, I know they keep telling us that we're about to move into the Pacific Century but I was rather hoping that the new master race would leave our golf courses alone. When they go, our civilisation crumbles.'

Clive Phelps developed his theme with well-informed rancour and I gave him his head. I came to understand Shohei

Ogino a little more and saw why he had selected me as his tame English golfer. Alan Saxon was a prominent figure in the world that he coveted. My name and my friendship would be a kind of passport for him and for his ambitions. I was not just there to make an instructional video with his financial backing. He wanted to use me.

Chiyo Takumi and her crew were set up and raring to go when we arrived at the practice green. Hideo Nakane was there to watch the filming and make any alterations to his commentary that became necessary. Both were eager to get under way again and—since I could only stay until the middle of the afternoon—I plunged straight in. Keiko had brought extra make-up to minimise the effect of the cuts and grazes down one side of my face and the mirror showed me that I no longer looked as if I had strayed off the set of the Hammer House of Horror. It gave me confidence. When I talked direct to camera about choosing a putter, I got most of it right on the first take. My director was delighted.

'Let's try it again, Alan.'

'The mixture as before?'

'With a little more attack, please.'

'Stand by.' Clearing my throat, I did my best to sound both relaxed and authoritative. 'The putter is the most important club in the bag so you choose it with the utmost care. Comfort is the watchword. You must have the right length of shaft and the right shaft-blade angle to suit your posture. Let me show you what I mean...'

It was a long morning but it paid handsome dividends. By dint of hard work and concentration, we got through pages of the script and felt the adrenalin pumping away. Lunch was forgotten as we moved on to some of the finer points of technique. What saved us so much time was the fact that I was on top form with my putter, sinking most of the short ones to order and achieving a healthy percentage of the longer ones. My last putt of the day was undoubtedly the best, a forty-footer across a sloping green. Since I was hitting the ball up to a cup

I could not properly see, the flagstick was used as a guide. I glanced up as a hand lifted it out of the hole then positioned it just behind my target so that it was pointing down like an arrow. Given such assistance, my putt was straight and true, rattling into the cup with the sweetest sound I'd heard since I'd come to Japan.

'Wonderful!' said Chiyo. 'That's it for today.'

'You were terrific, Alan,' agreed Hideo.

'Thanks.'

'After what you've been through, it's a miracle.' He turned to Chiyo. '*Mochi wa mochiya.*'

She laughed and nodded. I looked duly baffled.

Hideo smiled. 'Another old proverb. For rice cakes, go to the rice-cake maker.'

'Could you translate *that* as well?' I said.

'You're the right man for the job.'

They all concurred and Clive Phelps joined in the chorus of praise. I was just beginning to lap it all up when I heard a dissentient voice. It came from the young golfer who had completed his practice round and was walking past on his way back to the clubhouse. Fumio Ogino studied the scene with utter contempt, then fixed his gaze on me. Having tried to frighten me away, he found me continuing my work with renewed vigour. He stood very close as Japanese anger poured out of his mouth like molten lava.

I needed no translation.

He wanted to kill me.

Chapter Eight

Everyone thought that I was completely mad to charge off in order to catch the early evening flight to Bangkok but most of them at least humoured me. The predictable exception was Clive Phelps who reached new heights of vituperation, then demanded to know the cause of the emergency. When I kept him at arm's length, he was almost frothing at the mouth and he severed our friendship at least three times as he worked himself up into a real frenzy. There was no helping it. To confide in him would have been to expose myself to even greater ridicule because what I was really doing was to fly all that way on a hunch. Jumping through a narrow window of time, I might easily miss Sam Limsong altogether or—if we did actually connect—our meeting could well be fruitless. There were far too many imponderables. Clive would never understand.

Getting to Narita Airport turned out to be a major problem. Since we'd been told that the limousine was at our disposal while we were in Tokyo, I'd hoped to commandeer it for my own purposes and leave Clive to hitch a lift back to the city with the others. The chauffeur had his own ideas. When Hideo Nakane went over to acquaint him with the change in his travel plans, the man became quite heated and an argument ensued. We were too far away to hear much of what was said but the gesticulations were very eloquent. As the two men finished semaphoring away with their arms, Hideo came running across to me with an expression that was halfway between apology and annoyance.

'The driver won't take you,' he said.

'Why?'

'Something about having to be back in central Tokyo by a certain time. I think he's just being awkward.'

'Crack the whip over him.'

'I tried, Alan. He told me to take a powder.'

'Let *me* have a go at him.'

'No point. He doesn't speak English.' He grabbed my arm and pulled me towards the car park. 'Come on. Quick!'

'Where are we going?'

'*I'll* have to drive you.'

'That'd be fantastic! Sure you don't mind?'

'Of course not. In a crisis, all hands to the pumps.'

'I won't forget this, Hideo.'

'Only too glad to help.'

'Let me pay for the petrol at least.'

'No way, Alan. You are our guest.'

We reached his Mitsubishi and piled in. Hideo gunned the engine and we left the car park with a sense of real urgency. The vehicle was much smaller and less luxurious than the limousine but I didn't care about that. All that concerned me was the fact that I was getting my lift to the airport, after all. The friendly company was a bonus.

'What was the row about?' I wondered.

'Row?'

'With the chauffeur. All that pointing.'

'Oh, yes,' he said. 'I made the mistake of asking his advice about the quickest way. He was trying to send me on this long, complicated route around the city. It would never have got us there on time. I should've trusted to my own instincts all along. We should make it easily.'

'Good.'

'It may be a bumpy ride at times, though.'

'I can put up with anything.'

'If it gets too bad, just close your eyes.'

I soon found out what he meant. In order to drive me the seventy miles and more to the airport, Hideo had to get maximum speed out of his car on the clear stretches of road in order to make up for the delays in traffic. We positively hared along, zigzagging in and out of any other vehicles and breaking just about every rule in the Japanese highway code. When traffic thickened, Hideo did not stay meekly in his lane and wait for his turn in the queue. He would either somehow burrow his way through or swoop down off the expressway to flit in and out of suburban streets before rejoining it further along. His daredevil approach won us lots of enemies but it also gained valuable minutes.

'The secret is to keep on the move,' he said.

'Ideally, in one piece.'

He laughed. 'Am I going too fast?'

'You're the driver.'

'A little different from Carnoustie, I think?'

'With you at the wheel, she'd have a heart attack.'

'This is Tokyo. You must compete.'

He reinforced his point by cutting directly in front of a lorry. Glaring headlights flashed in his rear-view mirror. Traffic closed in from all sides to cut off his escape. We were stationary for over ten minutes and Hideo tapped his hands impatiently on the steering wheel. I went fishing for more information about the Ogino family. As usual, he was frank and forthcoming with much to say about Shohei and his three sons. I wondered where he drew the boundary line.

'You worked in the Ogino empire, didn't you?'

'Yes, Alan. Five and a half years.'

'Where?'

'At the headquarters. In Yokohama.'

'As a translator?'

'Principally.'

'What else?'

'Certain…special assignments.'

'Such as?'

'Shohei sent me to Europe a few times to look at some companies in which he was interested. He was very thorough.' He tossed me a smile. 'Call it research.'

'There is another name for it.'

'Business.'

'Were you responsible to Shohei himself?'

'Always.'

'So it was quite a high-powered position?'

'It paid well. While it lasted.'

'And why did it end?'

Another smile. 'I have too many scruples.'

'About what?'

'Let's leave it at that, Alan.'

'Did you fall out with the great man?'

'I'd never dare to do that. It would've been suicide.'

'Why?'

'You've seen the influence he could wield,' Hideo said. 'You don't get on the wrong side of a man like that.'

'Was he vindictive?'

'Extremely.'

'How far would he go to get his revenge?'

'All the way.'

We were on the move again and he needed full attention to wend his way through the crawling columns of traffic. After another foray into suburban Tokyo, the Mitsubishi fought for space on the expressway once more. The rush hour was making it impossible for anyone to hurry, let alone rush. I glanced at my watch and had my first lurching presentiment that we might not get to the airport in time. He stayed quietly optimistic.

'Don't give up, Alan.'

'There's still such a long way to go.'

'We'll make it somehow.'

'And if we don't?'

'I refuse even to consider that.'

'Attaboy!'

The more I got to know Hideo Nakane, the more I liked him but there was plainly a cut-off point in his ready supply of information. Loyalty to his ex-employer, and the fear that went with it, meant that there was a definite line which could never be crossed. I walked up and down it a few times to reconnoitre the other side.

'What sort of a boss will Takeshi make?'

'An effective one.'

'Is he as brutal as his father was?'

'He'll learn to be.'

'Would *you* work for him?'

'Takeshi has not asked me.'

'But if he did.'

'I think that's very unlikely.'

'Why?'

'Because I've…moved on now.'

I strolled along the border in the opposite direction.

'Did you see much of Yasayuki when you were there?'

'Oh, yes,' he said. 'The Research Department was in the same building. He was always about.'

'Doing what?'

'Controlling research projects.'

'Into what?'

'Potential areas of production.'

'Can you give me some examples?'

'Dozens, Alan. A multi-national company that size is advancing on several fronts at the same time. It has to in order to stay ahead of the game. Yasayuki's main concern has been the search for alternative sources of energy. And that work has become even more vital now.'

'Why?'

'The Gulf Crisis, of course. We import virtually all of our oil here. That makes us very vulnerable when trouble flares up in the Middle East.' He jabbed a foot down to dart into a gap between two buses. 'Look what happened in 1973. An Arab oil embargo that quadrupled the price. It nearly brought our country to its knees. That's when the search for other sources of power really began in earnest. Some of the biggest names in Japanese industry are involved—including Sumitomo, Yamaha and Toshiba.' He glanced around the interior of the car. 'And not forgetting Mitsubishi.'

'Or Ogino.'

'Exactly.'

'What form did Yasayuki's research take?'

'He's been looking at wind turbines, fuel cells and photo-voltaic converters, which use sunlight to produce electricity. Yasayuki designed a new type of solar panel that could put Ogino ahead of its rivals.'

'You seem to know a lot about it, Hideo.'

'I did some translation work in that area a couple of years ago. Shohei assigned me to the project.'

'What happens to it now?'

'That depends on Takeshi.'

'So it could falter?'

'Very easily.'

I waited until he had completed another death-defying piece of driving that took us a hundred yards further along the packed expressway. We were back to a crawl.

'What about Yasayuki's old speciality?'

'Speciality?'

'Electronic surveillance.'

'Ah.'

'Is he still interested in that?'

'I wouldn't know.'

'But Ogino manufactures stuff in that field.'

'Security is big business these days.'

'Is the Research Department working on that area?'

He shook his head. 'That's highly confidential.'

'All I want is a yes or no.'

'Sorry, Alan.'

'It's not a state secret, is it?'

But Hideo Nakane had told me all he was going to about the activities of the Ogino Corporation. Traffic was slowly building and his optimism began to fade a little. My own anxiety increased and I tried to ease it by making light conversation about our day's work at the course. During the next long and uncomfortable hour, we never even got out of first gear. Bangkok suddenly seemed an impossible distance away. I checked my watch and shuddered.

'We'll get there,' he said. 'We'll get there.'

'When?'

'Things will speed up in a while. You watch.'

Hideo was right but we were still only moving at thirty miles an hour. Even with frequent lane-changing, he could not find room to accelerate properly. I was frantic by the time we finally saw a clear outside lane. He responded like a rally driver and we threw caution to the winds, tearing along at eighty and using the horn to intimidate anyone who dared to get in our way. There was now an outside chance that we might get there in time but it would still be very close. Hideo's assurances soothed my raw nerve ends and I let my hopes swell when a sign told us we were only three kilometres from Narita Airport. Misfortune then struck.

After driving so well and so bravely for some three hours or more, Hideo made his first mistake. A long coach had lumbered into the outside lane to overtake a van that was in turn coasting past a sluggish lorry. There was no way through but Hideo was determined to create one. He sat on the tail of the van until it passed the lorry, then swung left into the inside lane in the hopes of passing the obstruction ahead of us. Boxed in by three vehicles, he braked sharply and swung on the steering wheel but he was out of luck. The Mitsubishi clipped the rear bumper of the car ahead and bounced off at an angle that sent it careering into the grass bank alongside the expressway. We hit the stump of a tree with a thud and stopped dead.

Neither of us was hurt but the car was clearly out of action for a long time. An almost tearful Hideo showered me with apologies but I didn't wait to hear them. Thanking him as I leapt out, I set off as fast as I could towards the airport. To get so close and then fail would be galling. I ignored the fire in my lungs, the drum inside my head and the sharp pain in my legs. I took no notice of the startled faces in the coaches that passed me. Forcing myself on, I kept a vision of Sam Limsong ahead of me and even managed an extra spurt over the last hundred yards. I barged in through the doors without ceremony and got an instant audience of passengers and officials. By the time I eventually reached the check-out desk, I was panting madly and barely able to ask for the ticket which was waiting for me. The girl looked at me with amused sympathy.

'No hurry, sir. Take-off delayed by thirty minutes.'

A Thai smile had never looked so sweet.

◇◇◇

Economy Class meant less comfort, less luxury and less room for my legs. It also meant that the food was less exciting and arrived more slowly but Thai International did not skimp on service. The cabin attendants gave me the same polite treatment I'd been accorded in First Class and not one of them blanched when they saw the damage that the bomb blast had done to the side of my face. I was a passenger and that entitled me to the highest standard of care. After the trauma of the car journey, it was wonderful to be wooed and waited upon. My complimentary orchid was never more welcome.

A free copy of *The Bangkok Post* gave me a somewhat different perspective on the Far East. Regular doses of *The Japan Times* and *The Daily Yomiuri* had accustomed me to headlines about the vexed question of whether or not troops should be sent to Iraq as part of the United Nations force. The issue split the government and the people to produce endless columns of newsprint. Only two items had managed to displace the story from a central position on the front pages. One was the Senkaku Islands dispute which had taken a new turn with China's outspoken attack on Japanese claims of sovereignty over the island chain. The other major news item was the murder of Shohei Ogino.

Thailand had problems of its own to report. Military police had been detached to Nakhon Si Thammarat to quell an anti-Government demonstration involving four thousand people and flooding around the capital was intensifying. *The Bangkok Post* also carried one of those life-is-like-that stories that would have delighted Clive Phelps with its potential implications. American importers had criticised Japanese condoms because they were too tight, too thin and too easily torn. Consumers were complaining that the product was not user-friendly. Here was one labour-saving device from the burgeoning superpower that had not met with universal acceptance.

It was a full-page advertisement in the paper that really captured my attention. 'Ancient Ayutthaya Was A Masterpiece of Classical Design,' I was informed. 'The Royal and Ancient Ayutthaya Sports Club Now Revives This Proud and Glorious Era.' A championship golf course had been built on the banks of the Chao Phya River, only an hour by private launch from Bangkok itself. Due to open in January 1991, it promised to be the most exclusive club in Thailand. My heart sank. Though I'm always pleased when a new golf course is opened, it grieves me if the game I love is used as a status symbol by the rich and privileged. Having had too much of it already in Japan, I baulked at the notion of exclusivity. The advertisement for Ayutthaya reminded me that I was still a conscience-stricken democrat.

One person who would be unhindered either by conscience or by principles of democracy was Sam Limsong who would certainly be playing in the inaugural tournament at the club. His talent set him above and apart from all the other golfers in Thailand and his nickname in some quarters of the sporting press was King of Siam. It was to the court of this ambiguous monarch that I was now hastening in a jumbo jet and I took the time to consider why. If my instincts had been sound, all the efforts I'd made would be worthwhile. Otherwise, I'd be involved in the most costly wild goose chase of my entire life.

My thesis was simple. A murder in Tokyo could only be explained by the relationship between a Thai golfer and the

Ogino family. What happened between them was a crucial factor in the equation. The ever-friendly Sam Limsong had shown a flash of real hatred when the name of Shohei Ogino was mentioned and the latter, by the same token, had revealed an antagonism towards him that obviously went deep. Fumio's belligerence had been more open and Mitsu had been visibly shaken by my reference to Sam Limsong as if guilty about the treatment meted out to him.

The bugging device was another critical element. I was now convinced that it had been placed in my bag for use solely while I was in Bangkok. There was no guarantee that it would get past the X-ray machine at the airport or the grievous bodily harm inflicted upon it by various baggage handlers along the way. Besides, if the object was to monitor my words and movements while I was in Japan, the device would have been fitted after I'd booked in at the Imperial Hotel. When I stumbled upon the object, my initial reaction had been one of anger and horror at the feeling that I was under surveillance but my indignation gradually faded away beneath the realisation that I was not the target for the device at all. Secured to the inside of my golf bag, all it would have picked up in my room at the Airport Hotel was a few brief and harmless phone calls. The real target was Sam Limsong.

Whoever planted the device knew in advance that I would be playing a round of golf with him. Our conversation in the locker room and around eighteen holes at The Rose Garden had been eavesdropped upon by an interested party. The bugging device was an Ogino product in every way. Why was it so important to keep track of what Sam Limsong might say to me as I spent a few pleasurable hours with him *en route* to Japan? Was someone afraid that he might let the cat out of the bag? Or was there another reason why someone had gone to such lengths to keep watch over him?

'More coffee, sir?'

'Oh, thank you.'

'Milk?'

'Just a touch.'

Having broken into my reverie, she moved on down the aisle to the next row of passengers. I became aware once more of the hit-or-miss nature of my venture. A delayed take-off at Narita Airport had already shortened my chances of a confrontation with Sam Limsong. His own flight was due to depart for Los Angeles just after midnight and that gave me a margin of little more than one hour. Delays in landing or in getting through Customs could shave vital minutes off that and there was always the possibility that Sam might arrive early at Bangkok Airport and go on through to its celebrated Duty Free shopping area before we had even touched down. Though traffic congestion would not detain us, the flight was just as harrowing as the car journey to Narita. The uncertainty was a continuous torment. I put my faith in the power of love. My fate rested in the hands of a beautiful Thai physiotherapist.

The inflight film was *A Shock to the System*, a dark comedy starring Michael Caine as a New York advertising executive who is supremely confident of getting a big promotion that is in the offing. When a hated rival is appointed instead of him, Caine has such a shock to the system that he determines to prove himself the better man. Since his bosses passed him over because they thought he lacked the killer instinct, that is what he demonstrates he has. A burdensome wife is first dispatched to her grave by the simple means of leaving her to put her hand on a live wire when she goes to mend a fuse in the cellar. Caine's rival is the next to fall to his electrical skills when his yacht is cunningly wired to explode. The rising executive rises on with a smile on his face. He is even able to bed the office lovely in order to provide himself with an alibi for one of the murders. The twist at the end is that there is no twist. Unlike most villains in most films, he actually gets away with it.

The subtle blend of fun and fantasy struck a number of chords in me. Disposing of a wife so easily was a subject that had great appeal. Rosemary has been killing me in stages over a number of years and it would be highly satisfying to get my own back, then walk free. The death of the rival awoke memories of the explosion at the Ogino household. In each case, a rich man was turning to a source of pleasure, whether yacht or cigar, when the bang came. In each case, the murderer remained at large though I suspected that our bomber did not have the wit or the panache of a Michael Caine. Cold, clinical and professional, he had given me a profound shock to the system. In flying away from him, I hoped to get a lot closer.

Tension mounted over the final hour until it was quite unendurable. I drank glass after glass of orange squash, I listened to music on my headphones, I prowled the gangway like a caged tiger but none of it helped. The prospect of failure was very real and very forbidding. Time was not on my side. Inevitable, a golfing metaphor intruded. Bangkok was the green and only a fluke shot helped me to reach it. The airport was the flagstick so I at least had something to aim at. What I lacked was the ball itself—Sam Limsong. I not only had to find him in the heavy rough of his travel plans, I had to putt with great accuracy to get the ball anywhere near the hole. It was the kind of problem you could never hope to explain on an instructional video.

As soon as we hit the runway, I was out of my seat belt and up on my feet. When we taxied to a halt, I was the first to get to the door. Unimpeded by any luggage, I was able to sprint out into the airport and along the echoing corridor. I was detained by Customs for less than a few minutes before coming out into the Arrivals Hall. Even at that late hour, it had its waiting horseshoe of relatives, friends and placarded chauffeurs, all of whom were taken aback when a tall, wild Englishman came loping out and headed towards the escalator. It was stationary when I got there but my foot activated it and I took the now moving steps in twos. Lurching out into the Departure Lounge, I collected even more stares but they did not deflect me for a second. A madcap journey of just under three thousand miles was crowned with success. He was there.

Sam Limsong was walking away from the check-out desk. My reasoning had been correct. The gorgeous Somjai had come to see him off and so he had delayed his departure until the last moment. Even a cursory glance told me how lucky my friend was in his choice of fiancée. Somjai was short but shapely with an unforced loveliness and a natural grace. Even amid the profusion of Thailand, her smile would win prizes and I was sorry to have to remove it for her. I ran across to them and slid the last few yards across the polished floor. Sam was astounded.

'Alan! What are you doing here?'

'Just happened to be passing.'

'Where did you come from?'

'Tokyo.'

'Why?'

'To see you.'

'But I'm just leaving.'

'You can give me five minutes, Sam.'

Somjai had been staring at the side of my face with evident alarm, wondering if I was a spectacularly careless shaver or if the dozens of tiny cuts had been put there in some other way. Sam felt obliged to introduce me to her but the name of Alan Saxon did not assuage her fears. She began to talk excitedly in her native language and he had to soothe her before we could continue. Leading Somjai to a seat, he glanced across at me with ill-concealed venom.

'Don't you think you owe this to me, Sam?' I said.

'No.'

'I've come a long way.'

'That's your problem.'

'Don't hold out on me.'

'I have a plane to catch.'

'You won't miss it.'

He looked at me, then at Somjai, then at me again. After a glance up at the clock in the hall, he came to a decision.

'Five minutes,' Alan.'

'You're on!'

'Upstairs.'

A reluctant Somjai stayed where she was as we took the escalator up to the next floor. We hurried to the café and sat at a table that overlooked the Departure Hall and gave Sam Limsong a view of his fiancée. His friendship with me did not soften the brusque tone.

'What the hell are you playing at?' he demanded.

'I had to see you.'

'When I'm with Somjai? This is not a good time.'

'It was all I had.'

'Then say your piece and let me go.'

'Hold on, hold on,' I told him. 'It's not as easy as that. We're into something really serious here, Sam. Have you forgotten that Shohei Ogino was murdered?'

'No, I haven't. I give thanks for it every day.'

'Why?'

'That's my business.'

'Supposing I'd been killed with him. Would you have given thanks for that as well?'

'No, of course not.'

'Then help me.'

'Look, Alan…'

'Make up your mind which side you're on.'

He glanced down at the anxious, upturned face of Somjai and bit his lip. Embarrassment was written all over him. I was not there to spare his feelings and so I pressed hard.

'Come on, Sam,' I urged. 'Stop holding out on me. I'm up to my neck in this. You can't just bugger off to the States and leave me stranded. I've been blown up, I've been followed and I've been threatened. *You* know why. So tell me.'

'I know nothing about that explosion,' he said quickly.

'Just give me the reason behind it.'

'I don't know that either.'

'You're lying, Sam.'

'I'm not, honestly. All I can tell is that Shohei Ogino was a very nasty man. Oh, he was polite and civilised on the surface—his type always are. But once he took against you, he could be a monster.'

'You obviously speak from bitter experience.'

'I do, believe me!'

'Go on.'

'That bastard made me pay!'

'For what?'

'It's over now.'

'For *what*, Sam?'

'Something I'd prefer to forget.'

'I have to get to the bottom of this.'

'It's best left buried.'

'Maybe this'll change your mind.'

I brought the bugging device out of my pocket and slapped it down on the table in front of him. Recognising what it was at once, he glared across at me.

'Where did you find this?'

'Hidden away inside my golf bag,' I said. 'It was planted there while I was staying in Bangkok so that someone could listen in to what you and I were talking about at The Rose Garden. Now who'd do a thing like that, eh? Any ideas? Who is so keen to keep tabs on Sam Limsong?'

'They never leave go!' he said ruefully.

'They?'

'It goes on and on.'

'Are you talking about Shohei and Fumio?'

He took a deep breath, glanced down at the watching Somjai again then fixed me with a grim stare. There was no trace now of the amiable smile and the raised straw trilby. Sam Limsong was being forced to remember something which he had hoped to leave in the past. It had returned to haunt him and to threaten his future happiness.

'Listen to me, Alan,' he said. 'I have a good life. I work hard at my game, I make lots of money, I'm about to get married. Somjai is a wonderful girl and I don't want anything to come between us. You understand?' I nodded. 'If I tell the truth, it goes no futher than this table. Okay?'

'You have my word, Sam.'

'Shohei Ogino had a reason to hate me.'

'Because you usually keep Fumio in his place?'

'That's only part of it. Fumio is a very talented golfer but he will not have the edge over me for a long time. I'll always stay ahead of him.'

'Yet he beat you in that play-off.'

He spoke through gritted teeth. 'That was afterwards. It was not a fair fight. There's no surprise that he beat me. The wonder is that I even reached the play-off. It was only pride that kept me going in that tournament.'

'Had Shohei been leaning on you.'

'Very hard.'

'Why?'

'Because of Mitsu.' Without daring to look down at his fiancée, he plunged on. 'It happened while she was studying in Boston. We became friends and then it took off in a big way. I…saw a lot of her. We were very discreet. We had to be, Alan. Think of the situation. I am not just her brother's biggest rival. I am a Thai. To someone like Shohei, that is like being an outcast. In his eyes, I was not fit even to touch Mitsu. We had to be extra careful.'

'So how did he find out?'

'With one of these.' He picked up the bugging device. 'Shohei had her tailed by a private detective. He caught us.' Sudden anger seized him. 'What sort of a man does that, Alan? What sort of a father has his daughter *watched*?'

'Were there repercussions?'

'The worst kind.' He stood up and thrust the metallic object back into my hand. 'And it looks like they're still going on. I want no more of it. I'm finished.'

He stalked off towards the escalator. Somjai was out of her seat at once and running across to greet him. I was eager for more detail but knew I would have to settle for what I had already squeezed out of him. Sam Limsong had left one life behind him at the top of the escalator and he was now embracing another in the Departure Hall. He had given me the breakthrough that I'd sought. One unexpected name had solved many small puzzles and taken me closer to a solution of the big puzzle. Mitsu Ogino was the catalyst. She and I would need to have a much longer talk together.

My return flight was due to depart in an hour. I checked in and joined the queue to get through Customs. In reaching Bangkok Airport, I'd got closer to the flagstick than I'd imagined. My short putt had rattled into the cup.

The ball was dead.

◇◇◇

I slept all the way back to Tokyo and the considerate cabin attendants did not disturb me. My facial injuries were made to look worse by a day's growth of beard but I was allowed into Japan with the usual politeness. On the two-hour coach journey back to my hotel, I dozed off again. There was an urgent message waiting for me when I picked up my key at the reception desk. Takeshi Ogino wished to speak to me on his private number. He was now the head of the family and the man who controlled my stay in his country. He might also prove to be a useful ally against his younger brother. I wondered how much he had been involved in the persecution of Sam Limsong.

Chiyo Takumi had been alarmed at the news of my trip to Bangkok but she had been mollified by my promise to be back at the course for another filming session by late morning. A restorative bath was thus at the top of my list and I went straight up to my room to have it. While the bath was filling, I rang the number left by Takeshi. He was not available at that moment but his secretary had been briefed to invite me to dine with him that evening. When the details had been agreed, I took to the water for some horizontal luxury. Half an hour floated dreamily past. I was just hauling myself out of the tub when I heard the knock on the door to my room. Pulling on a bath robe, I stepped out to put an eye to the peep-hole in the door. A young man was waiting with a deferential smile.

'Who is it?' I asked.

'I come to give you Japanese massage.'

'But I didn't order one.'

'Your friend order it for you. Mr Phelps.'

'Clive?'

'He think you need after long flight.'

It made sense. Twelve hours in the air had put their shares of aches and pains into my body. Clive wanted me at my best when I got to the course and a massage was the ideal way to ease tight muscles. The young man was dressed in much the same outfit as my previous masseur. Sensing my hesitation, he bowed and made to go.

'You no need me, I leave you alone.'

'Wait,' I said. 'Since you're here…'

'Thank you, sir.'

I let him in and he put the DO NOT DISTURB sign on the door knob outside. He seemed quite happy to massage me through the bath robe and indicated that I should lie down on the bed. I took up a position on my left side and waited for the probing fingers to begin. Like his predecessor, he knelt beside me and began to work first on my neck and shoulders. As he pushed and kneaded away, he gradually increased the pressure and checked the result.

'This hurt?'

'No, no,' I said.

'You tell me if too hard.'

'I will, don't worry.'

He angled himself to get a better purchase, straddling me so that he could concentrate on the back of my head. He poked away with such insidious precision that it felt as if he was reaching inside my skull to pinch then caress my brain. The old mixture of pain and pleasure was slowly lulling me to sleep. I was just about to yield myself up when the agony started. It was as if someone was inserting a thick needle into my skull from just behind my right ear. As I stiffened to resist, the needle went in deeper.

'That hurts!' I yelled.

'Sorry.'

'Stop it at once!'

'Sorry.'

'Get off!'

But he had me totally under control now. Pressing hard with a thumb behind and below my ear, he was causing me such intense pain that I flailed away to try to dislodge him. He imprisoned me in an expert arm-lock then adjusted his feet to get a firmer hold on my body. I bucked and reared and did all I could to shift him but he had me completely in his power now. He was a professional and I was quite helpless. My shouts of protest soon turned to hoarse whispers as he applied even more pressure and wrung the last few drops of energy out of me as if squeezing a sponge dry.

I made one last effort to get him off my back but he simply tightened his grip all over. His thumb forced me closer and closer towards unconsciousness. Here was no thoughtful suggestion by Clive Phelps. Someone else had sent this particular masseur along to me with special orders. I was still trying to decide who that someone might be when the torment finally ceased and everything suddenly went very dark.

Chapter Nine

Darkness brought both rest and comfort. I was out cold for well over an hour but when I came to, I felt oddly refreshed. There was a dull pain behind my ear where the thumb had carried out its drilling operations but I was otherwise strangely restored by my enforced nap. I could move freely and seemed to have suffered no further damage at the hands of my fake masseur. When I got up and checked my appearance in the mirror, my face was showing nothing worse than the effects of a long flight. I rubbed my neck to ease the pain but the memory of what had happened still smarted. In the one place where I'd felt really safe, I'd been overpowered and rendered senseless. It was unnerving.

This second warning had the autograph of Fumio Ogino all over it. After threatening me with Crew Cut, he had unleashed a more subtle and dangerous enemy. It was his way of saying that he could—and would—have me killed if necessary. I was highly vulnerable and the Japanese massage had been graphic proof of the fact. My association with Shohei Ogino and his younger son was less than happy. On two separate occasions now, I'd been lucky to escape with my life. The visitor to my hotel room was every bit as lethal as the exploding cigar box. When I looked for reassurance from other members of the family, it was not forthcoming. Preoccupied with his researches, Yasayuki had no time for an imported golfer with a contract to make an instructional video, and his elder brother, Takeshi—though nominally on my

side—was a rather chilling individual caught up in the politics of
big business. Mitsu was not even speaking to me.

There was nowhere to turn.

'Open up, Saxon! I know you're in there.'

'Be with you in a tick.'

'Get a move on, man! We're late.'

'Don't be so impatient.'

'Let's have some urgency around here!'

'Relax, Clive.'

'What are you doing in there?' he demanded. 'More to the
point—who *with*?'

'Nobody.'

'Pull the other one!'

'She won't let me.'

'Open up!' he yelled, pounding on the door. 'I have a search
warrant. Open in the name of the law!'

When I unlocked the door, Clive Phelps almost fell into my
arms. Brushing past me, he charged straight across to the bed in
the hope of finding a naked woman in a post-coital haze amid
the rumpled sheets. Disbelief made him splutter.

'This bed hasn't even been slept in!'

'We did it standing up.'

'You're a washout, Saxon!'

'Sorry, Clive.'

'What do you *do* for sex?' he wailed.

'I play golf.'

'Don't you ever get a hard-on?'

'Only when I sink a thirty-foot putt.'

He hurled a vicious pillow at me but I ducked beneath it,
grabbed some clothes then dived into the bathroom. A stout
lock kept him at bay while I got dressed. Clive used his fists to
beat out a tattoo on the bathroom door.

'What about Bangkok?' he said.

'It's the capital of Thailand.'

'Why did you go there?'

'To speak to Sam Limsong.'

'Couldn't you have rung him up instead?'

'He wasn't answering my calls.'

'Did he say why?'

'Eventually.'

'Well?'

'It's a secret.'

'Fucking hell!'

'All will become clear in due course.'

'I want to know *now*.'

'You'll have to wait.'

'Why?'

'It's another secret.'

'Christ Al-bloody-mighty!'

'I knew you'd take it in the right spirit.'

'Stop doing this to me!' he roared.

'Then practise a little self-control.'

'Honestly, Saxon—I could *murder* you!'

I opened the door. 'Wait your turn in the queue.'

Before he could resume his invective, I told him about the unsolicited visit from the masseur. Clive was highly alarmed by the incident, all the more so because his own name had been used in the deception. He wanted instant retribution.

'Give the manager a bollocking,' he urged.

'What for?'

'Letting you in for that ordeal. His staff are supposed to serve the guests, not attack them.'

'This man was not a genuine member of the staff.'

'Then hotel security is to blame. Give *them* a roasting. For God's sake, man, this is serious! You don't expect to stay in a five-star luxury and have a trained psychopath dropping in to give you a massage. Complain!'

'There's no point, Clive.'

'There's every point,' he argued. 'If I'd been put in that kind of danger, I'd be yelling my protest from the rooftop. Apart from anything else, it will keep the security people on their toes and ensure that it won't happen again.'

'It won't *need* to happen again.'

'What are you on about?'

'Tactics. Next time will be different. And final.'

'That's why you must have protection. Wake up, Saxon. Get angry. Don't take this lying down.'

'I had no option.'

'And call the police at once.'

'No way.'

'But you must report this.'

'I'm not bringing the police in.'

'Can't you forget your hang-ups just this once?'

'I fight my own battles.'

'You can't handle this on your own.'

'Forewarned is forearmed.'

'Have you taken leave of your senses?' he said. 'You're a target. You need all the help you can get.'

'I'll stick close to you,' I teased.

'Call the coppers!'

'I don't trust them.'

'They're not all as bad as your father.'

'Most of them are worse.'

'We're talking survival here.'

'I have no worries on that score.'

'So what's the master plan?'

'I'll do it my way.'

Clive lifted both hands high in a gesture of despair.

'That's all we need,' he said. 'Frank Fucking Sinatra!'

◇◇◇

Hideo Nakane was waiting for us downstairs to thumb a lift to the Wada International Country Club and to brief us on the day's filming. He was mortified by his failure to get me to the airport on the previous day but delighted to hear that I had actually caught my flight to Bangkok. His own car was now undergoing repairs and would be off the road for a week and so he shared our limousine for the drive west. His presence was an incidental bonus because it prevented Clive Phelps from interrogating me too closely about all that I had found out in the previous twelve hours. By the same token, Clive helped to smother Hideo's own curiosity about my emergency dash to Thailand and I was able to get away with a few neutral comments. Since they patently cancelled each other out, I resolved to travel to and fro in a threesome whenever possible. It was easier on the nerve ends.

When we reached the course itself, Hideo really came into his own. He handled the club officials with firmness and diplomacy, he calmed down irate members who wanted to use the practice green which we monopolised and he made himself useful in a hundred unobtrusive ways during the filming itself. He also did his best to keep morale high with an endless stream of compliments and words of encouragement. I was particularly struck with the way that he treated Chiyo Takumi, who was rather morose and preoccupied when we first arrived. Hideo got to work at once with quiet assurance and he soon coaxed the first smile of the day from her. Buoyed up by his support, Chiyo tackled the schedule with her usual blend of flair and commitment, drawing the best out of us all in the limited time at her disposal.

One of the few positive benefits of Shohei Ogino's death was the fact that it absolved me from my ancillary duties with the business community. Instead of having to play some obligatory rounds of golf with his friends and colleagues—eighteen holes of statutory boredom in a foreign language—I was able to give my full concentration to the making of the video. All of us got extra value from the enterprise because it enabled us to shake off the horrors of the past week and lose ourselves in a game that we loved. It was our escape hatch.

Keiko used her make-up brush to banish all traces of jet lag from my face and to conceal my injuries, but it was the camera that was my greatest ally. Since the day was devoted to bunker shots and awkward lines, it was the ball itself that dominated the screen. It lay half buried in sand, it nestled in thick grass, it hid beneath twigs, it clung to the base of a tree trunk, it sunbathed at the water's edge, it found mud, hollow and gradient. Equipped with my clip-on microphone, I talked my way through a variety of retrieval shots, always emphasising the position of my feet and the angle of the club face at the moment of impact. Alan Saxon was heard but rarely seen. Filming speeded up accordingly.

Lunch was a tuna sandwich and a Diet Coke, hastily consumed while the cameras were being set up for the next shot; indeed, there was a hand-to-mouth air to the whole session which made for real excitement. Chiyo was thrilled to have so much useable footage in the can and she seemed to have shrugged off her earlier mood entirely. There was no hint of her brooding silence as she egged us on to complete one last sequence before the light started to fade.

'Play to the camera, Alan,' she urged.

'Ready when you are.'

'See if you can strike gold first time.'

'That's a tall order, Chiyo.'

'You can do it.'

'I'll try.'

But my hopes were very slim. The final shot of the day was a chip-and-run from the mild rough that fringed the green and it was designed to show how to take advantage of the flagstick. When a player's ball is not on the putting surface, he has the right to ask that the flagstick be left in the hole where it can occasionally act as a buffer to stop the ball near the cup. I demonstrated the other possible advantage. A delicate chip with a 5-iron sent the ball on to the green and straight on towards the flagstick which it struck with a *ping* before dropping sweetly into the hole. The shot owed more to outrageous luck than to skill but it brought cheers from the whole crew and provided a high note on which to end. I acknowledged the mini-ovation with a regal wave then offered to buy everyone a drink in the clubhouse.

Over a glass of Sapporo beer, I spoke alone with Chiyo.

'Satisfactory day?' I said.

'Best so far.'

'We may actually complete this video then.'

She was serious. 'We must, Alan. It's a sacred trust.'

'I wouldn't go that far.'

'I would.' She relaxed and smiled. 'Besides, we're all professionals. We like to do a job properly.'

'Every shot perfectly hit.'

'That last one, especially. A touch of real magic.'

'I can still turn it on now and again.'

'That's why you were hired. You have quite a reputation in Japan, you know. Golfers here have long memories.'

Her smile faded and her eyelids flickered nervously.

'Is everything okay?' I said.

'Yes. Fine, thanks.'

'Are you sure?'

'Of course.'

A token shrug. 'I had the feeling that you were a bit distracted earlier on, that's all. As if you had…something on your mind.'

'I do,' she conceded. 'Finishing this video.'

'Anything else?'

'Alan, there's no *time* for anything else.'

'That's true.'

'This means so much to me.'

Before she could explain why, Clive Phelps ambled across with a drink in his hand and slipped into Chat-Up Mode. A week of consistent failure had not deterred him and he made fresh overtures to Chiyo. She was amused but far too evasive for him and he suddenly found himself talking to thin air. Clive gave me a broad wink.

'She's playing hard to get.'

'That's not how it looks from here.'

'I know women,' he asserted. 'I have a sixth sense.'

'For what?'

'The delights of the flesh.'

'Don't you ever think of anything *else*, Clive?'

'Yes—a nice cheroot straight afterwards.'

It was time to head back. We collected my golf bag then joined Hideo in the rear of the limousine. As we set off, I noticed

that we had a change of chauffeur. He had the same hat and
uniform as his colleague but he possessed wider shoulders and
a thicker neck. Before I could take a further inventory, I was
hauled into a discussion of the relative merits of Japanese and
Thai women. It resolved itself largely into a monologue by Clive
Phelps but his fulsome praise of Bangkok maidenry met with
some spirited resistance from Hideo. Our translator was fiercely
loyal to Japanese notions of beauty and quite scathing about Thai
standards. I'd never heard him speak with such contempt about
anything and I was quite taken aback, but Clive immediately
tried to harness his inside knowledge.

'What about Chiyo?' he asked. 'Is *she* attractive?'

'Very.'

'Classic Oriental features?'

'She is a typical Japanese woman.'

'Does she have a regular boyfriend?'

'I don't think so.'

'You and she are not, by any chance…?'

'No, no, of course not,' said Hideo. 'That would be out of
the question. We are colleagues. It would not even enter my
mind. Chiyo would consider it to be an insult.'

'Oh.'

'I'm sure you feel the same about her, Clive.'

'Yes, yes,' he lied.

'We owe Chiyo the utmost respect.'

'No doubt about it. She's a real pro and I have the greatest admiration for what she's done and the way she's done it.
Frankly, I'm amazed to find a woman involved in a project like
this at all. When she's got the job strictly on merit—as Chiyo
obviously did—it's even more creditable. She doesn't have a
bigger fan than me, Hideo.' Clive turned to whisper in my ear.
'But does she fuck?'

We talked golf for the rest of the journey. Hideo was first out
of the car when we got back and Clive was just behind him. They
sauntered off into the hotel, leaving me to pick up my golf bag.
As the chauffeur hauled it out of the car boot, I caught my first

glimpse of his face. It was large, flat and ugly with pitted skin. He lifted his hat to aid identification and the close-cropped hair left no room for doubt. Crew Cut had driven us back from the course. He handed me my clubs and gave me the malign grin of a man who enjoys springing unpleasant surprises.

His voice hit my ear like a knuckleduster.

'Have a nice day,' he said.

◇◇◇

Superintendent Akio Ushiba of the Tokyo Metropolitan Police did something that I would never have believed possible until it actually happened, and I could only explain it away in terms of the intense pressure I was under. He made me glad to see a policeman. There was something curiously reassuring about the beaming face, the throaty chuckle and the beefy handshake, perhaps because they were so unexpected. When I went off to dine with Takeshi Ogino that evening, I had no idea that Ushiba would be there as well. The three of us met up in a private room in an exclusive restaurant in the Ginza area. Takeshi wore a beautifully tailored dark blue suit and exuded a sense of well-behaved authority but it was his stocky companion who really caught my eye. Superintendent Ushiba was an uncomfortably welcome sight.

When the opening pleasantries were over, we exchanged our shoes for pairs of slippers then adjourned to the low table that stood on a dais in the corner of the room. The others settled happily into their seats but I knew that I would not be able to maintain my cross-legged position for long. Ushiba spotted my problem at once.

'Stretch your legs under the table,' he said.

'I will.'

'We'd like you to be completely at your ease.'

'Thanks.'

He waited while I adjusted my position then tossed a casual question over the top of the menu he was consulting.

'Why did you walk to the restaurant?'

'It was so close to the hotel.'

'But Takeshi sent a car to pick you up.'

'I felt like some fresh air.'

I was also anxious to break out of the Bad Chauffeur Syndrome that was plaguing me. One driver had refused to take me to Narita Airport, a second—Hideo Nakane—had involved us in a road accident and the third had a hairstyle to which I took serious exception. Unless checked now, this kind of thing could be habit-forming so I went for the safe option of finding out where the restaurant was and getting there on foot. Both men clearly saw this as an example of English eccentricity.

Takeshi Ogino was as expressionless as ever but Akio Ushiba was relaxed and jocular. Nobody would have taken him for a man at the head of a murder investigation. There was no hint of the enormous strain that he must be under, no sign that the routine media pounding was getting to him. I tried to penetrate his surface affability.

'Have you made any progress, Superintendent?'

'Considerable progress.'

'The papers don't seem to think so.'

'That is their privilege.'

'Do you have any idea who is behind it all?'

'We are narrowing down our list of suspects.'

'Is there any possibility of an arrest?'

'Eventually.'

'How much longer will it take?'

'The net is tightening all the time.'

'But is there anybody in it?' I said pointedly.

He gave a hearty laugh. 'We hope so, Alan, or we'll be made to look very foolish. The Tokyo Metropolitan Police have a high success rate when it comes to solving murders. I'll make sure that success continues.'

'Good.'

'Be patient just a little longer.'

A waiter shuffled into the room and bowed. Takeshi and Ushiba gave him his orders while I stared in dismay at the

Japanese characters in my menu and wished that Hideo was on hand to provide English subtitles. Ushiba came to my rescue.

'I've taken the liberty of ordering for you,' he said.

'Thanks. What am I getting?'

'An interesting selection of traditional dishes.'

'I'll try anything once.'

'What are you like with chopsticks?'

'Hopeless.'

'I thought you might be. That's why I asked the waiter to bring a fork for you. Eating with chopsticks is an art.'

It was not one that I would ever master and I was pleased when the waiter reappeared with my fork. He also brought three glasses of warm *sake* and I drank mine with undisguised relish. Ushiba waited until I'd finished.

'Why did you go to Bangkok?' he asked.

'What?'

'Yesterday evening. You went on a Thai International flight and returned early this morning. It's a long way to go for such a short time, isn't it?'

'I had to see someone.'

'Yes, I guessed that much, Alan. Who was it?'

'A friend.'

'Male or female?'

'Does it matter?'

'You tell me.'

Ushiba's smile had a steely quality now and he was not going to be shaken off easily. Takeshi was also watching me intently as if hoping that I'd be caught out. The cosy meal had taken on a slightly oppressive quality and I needed to create some breathing space. I fell back on bluff.

'It was a young woman.'

'She must be someone special.'

'Very special.'

'European?'

'Oriental.'

'I applaud your taste and admire your devotion.'

'It was the only time I could see her.'

'Why?'

'Problems. With her father.'

'Ah.'

'One fleeting moment was all we had.'

A nudging grin flowered. 'Was it worthwhile?'

'Of course!'

He chuckled and the ghost of a smile haunted Takeshi's lips. They found the idea of a romantic gesture on my part rather diverting and so I added a few decorative flourishes to the story to give it more credence. Taken in by my patent sincerity, neither of them realised that the female who had made my journey to Bangkok so productive was Mitsu Ogino. The meal was served and the subject was dropped but I stayed very much on the alert. It was not only in Thailand that I'd been kept under surveillance.

Akio Ushiba deployed his chopsticks with great skill and I was mesmerised by the way that they knitted intricate patterns in the air. After an abortive attempt to copy him, I reached for the fork with gratitude. The food was served on trays in a series of small china dishes and it was quite delicious. Though I had no idea what I was eating, I enjoyed every mouthful. Ushiba somehow managed to stay in control while showing all due deference to our host. After pushing around a few neutral topics of conversation, he brought his investigation back into focus.

'The last time we met, I mentioned a golf course.'

'Packwood Heath,' I recalled.

'Takeshi confirms his father's interest in it.'

'Yes,' said the other, taking his cue. 'My father had a lifelong wish to own a course in England and he searched for a suitable property for many years. We knew that he was trying to start negotiations for this Packwood Heath but we had no details.' He fixed me with a level gaze. 'My father was a very secretive man, Mr Saxon. Some things he liked to handle by himself. Even his sons were kept in the dark.'

'Why was that?' I wondered.

'It was his—how do you say…?'

'Style.'

'Thank you, Mr Saxon. His style.'

Ushiba resumed. 'Shohei's private papers would have told us much more but they were destroyed in the bomb blast so we have had to piece the story together bit by bit.'

'What about Fumio?' I suggested. 'He's the golfer. Surely he was in on his father's scheme.'

'Fumio knows no more than me,' said Takeshi sharply.

'That seems unlikely.'

'You must take my word for it.'

'We rang Packwood Heath itself,' said Ushiba, 'but they were not at all helpful. English people give nothing away. They admitted that they knew of a Shohei Ogino but that is all I could get out of them. They were very touchy.'

'I can imagine,' I said.

'A pity you were not at my side, Alan.'

'Why?'

'To talk to them over the telephone.'

'I can't promise that I'd have gleaned anything more than you did, Superintendent. Course managements are like secret societies. Outsiders don't get a look-in.'

'Tell us about the place,' he invited.

'Packwood Heath?'

'What sort of a club is it? What sort of an area? How far is it from London? Tell us everything you know, however trivial it may seem. Where exactly *is* Packwood Heath?'

I gave them as full an account as I could, drawing on some of the facts that had arisen during my discussion of the course with Clive Phelps and understanding, even as I spoke, what a tempting proposition the club could be to a foreign buyer. They traded several meaningful glances and were obviously hearing exactly what they had expected. It all served to reinforce Ushiba's earlier suspicion.

'Shohei wished to discuss Packwood Heath with you.'

'For what reason?'

'So that you might help him.'

'In what way?'

He gave a wry smile. 'We may never know.'

When the meal was over, Ushiba excused himself and got up to leave us. As he put his shoes back on, he introduced a gentle note of warning.

'Inform us of any other travel plans,' he said.

'Travel plans?'

'Wild dashes to meet special ladies.'

'Ah, yes. Bangkok.'

'We need to be aware of your movements. It's the only way we can make sure that nothing unpleasant happens to you. Believe it or not, Japanese police are on your side.'

'That's what worries me.'

He slapped his thigh and guffawed. After waving his thanks to Takeshi, he went out still rocking with mirth. Superintendent Akio Ushiba was the most dangerous policeman I'd ever met. He made me like him.

Left alone at last with me, my host plunged straight in.

'I brought you here to apologise, Mr Saxon,' he said. 'And to give you my personal assurance that everything will be done to make the remainder of your stay in Tokyo as pleasant as possible.'

'That might be tricky in the circumstances.'

'I know and I am deeply sorry that my family has been the cause of so much upset to you. The important thing is that your contract is honoured and that your video is made. It was a project that was dear to my father's heart. We are all anxious to see it completed.'

'Does that include Fumio?'

'It includes the whole Ogino family.'

'Try telling that to your younger brother.'

'Fumio will respect his father's wishes.'

'That's not the impression I got.'

'What do you mean?'

'We had a little chat about the video,' I explained. 'Your brother was less than supportive.'

'Ignore him,' said Takeshi peremptorily. 'I speak for the family now and my decision has been made. You will have all the assistance you need to finish your work here. If you have any trouble at all, contact me on my direct line.'

He handed me a business card which was printed in English on the reverse side. I noted that he was now the President of the corporation. It had not taken him long to formalise his elevation. Throughout his empire, the name of Shohei Ogino had probably already been shunted off the headed notepaper. Takeshi had moved with the eagerness of someone who had waited a long time for this moment. Power had turned a subdued and colourless individual into a man of action who was now glistening with self-assurance. He began to preen himself.

'I intend to fulfil all my father's ambitions…'

Takeshi Ogino talked openly about his plans for the future development of the corporation and allowed himself a few personal boasts along the way. Instead of furthering someone else's ambitions, he was clearly set on pursuing his own with the quiet ruthlessness that was the family trait. He was also reminding me with polite forcefulness of Japan's superiority over the ailing economies of countries like my own. I was getting financial intimidation by way of dessert. Keen to learn all I could about his business operations, I fed him questions to draw out further details, noting how often he mentioned himself and how rarely he referred to his brothers. At no stage did he even acknowledge that he possessed a sister.

Listening to him made me appreciate the root difference between the two funerals that I'd recently attended. Aunt Enid had robbed the whole family of its vital spark and left it debilitated. The death of Shohei Ogino, by contrast, had liberated his family. They had suddenly come alive. Sons who had tamely obeyed his dictates were now showing that they had minds of their own. Fumio had been the first to throw his weight about and Yasayuki had come decisively out of his shell but it was Takeshi whose transformation had been most dramatic. Weeks before one official enthronement, another new emperor had already crowned himself.

I found a way to halt his stately procession.

'What's your opinion of Sam Limsong?' I asked.

He lapsed back at once into a watchful silence. When he finally spoke, it was with an icy neutrality.

'I have no opinion.'

'Your father and he fell out.'

'Did they?'

'You must know why.'

'It was a matter between the two of them.'

'Your father surely confided in you.'

'That is my business, Mr Saxon.'

He got up from the table to signal the end of the meal and I rose to my feet as well. My height advantage was neutralised by his air of total control. He mixed politeness and contempt in equal proportions.

'I'm not interested in Thai golfers,' he said. 'To be frank with you, I'm not all that interested in golf itself. It was my father's obsession not mine and so we will not be pursuing this idea of buying a course in England. When you get home, you may tell your friends at Packwood Heath that they are safe from Japanese invasion.' He sized me up before continuing. 'This instructional video is another matter. It's a business undertaking that must be seen through. An Ogino contract is a solemn bond. Besides, Mr Saxon...' A thin smile hovered. 'I have another reason for wanting you to proceed with your work over at Wada.'

I knew what it was. Takeshi was enjoying the discomfort that my presence in Tokyo was giving to Fumio. By keeping me there as the resident golfing star, he could use me as a weapon against his younger brother. Every time I smiled at the camera, I was striking a blow in a family feud.

'May I offer you a lift back to your hotel?' he said.

'I'll walk, thanks.'

'You know where to reach me if you need me. Feel free to ask for any favour.'

'There is one, as it happens.'

'Well?'

'Transport to and from the golf course.'

'What about it?'

'I'd prefer a woman driver.'

He was utterly baffled.

◇◇◇

The Imperial Hotel was less than ten minutes away and I walked briskly through the neon-lit streets of the Ginza. I was in the city's smartest and most fashionable district with glittering department stores and exquisite little shops on every side of me but I only saw one thing in the windows that I passed. It was the reflection of the man who was following me at a discreet distance on the opposite pavement. All that I could establish was that he was short, slim and wearing a dark suit. I could pick out no facial features nor put an age to him. The man posed no physical threat to me. He was just a rather irritating burden that I was dragging along on the end of an invisible piece of elastic.

When the hotel came in sight, I strolled in through the main entrance then went quickly across to one of the large windows to take a proper look at my shadow. He was a well-dressed man in his thirties with an intelligent face and questing eyes. After checking his watch, he turned back to the road and gestured with a hand. Seconds later he was being driven away in a police car. Superintendent Akio Ushiba was indeed watching over me.

I cruised the lounge to make sure that nobody else was keeping an eye on me then I went up to my room. As soon as I stepped out of the lift, I sensed danger and I brought my arms up to defend myself as a figure stepped abruptly out of a doorway. It was the last person I'd expected.

'I'm so glad to see you, Alan!'

'What are *you* doing here?'

'I'm frightened. We must talk.'

'Come right in.'

I opened the door and took Chiyo Takumi into my room.

Chapter Ten

She was pale and trembling so I took her across to the sofa then opened the mini-bar to pour her a glass of brandy. It soothed her nerves and brought a nod of gratitude. I helped myself to a tonic water before sitting beside her. Chiyo took my hand for comfort and squeezed it hard. I gave her plenty of time to compose herself. Eventually, she managed a shrug of apology.

'Sorry, Alan.'

'For what?'

'Bursting in on you like this.'

'You're more than welcome, Chiyo,' I said. 'I'll do all I can to help, you know that. Just tell me what the problem is. Did you say you were frightened?'

'Very frightened.'

'Of what?'

She finished off the brandy then took a deep breath.

'It began with a phone call this morning,' she said. 'A man's voice warned me not to turn up for filming today or there'd be big trouble.'

'Did he specify?'

'All too clearly. He said that I'd end up in the same boat as Shohei.' She had another fit of trembling for a few seconds. 'He put it more crudely than that.'

'In Japanese?'

'Yes.'

'What did you do?'

'Just sat there and shivered with fear.'

'And then?'

'I rang the police to report the call. Superintendent Ushiba was not available but one of his men took down the details and said he'd pass them on in case they were relevant to the investigation. Hell!' She winced at the memory. 'I needed help there and then. Some weirdo is making threats down the telephone at me and all the police can do is talk about whether it's relevant or not!'

'You obviously decided to brave it out.'

'What else could I do?'

'Run off and hide. As most people would've done.'

'I couldn't let the rest of you down, Alan.'

'That's very noble, Chiyo, but there are times when you should put personal safety first.' I slipped a consoling arm around her. 'No wonder you were so distracted earlier on.'

'I was beside myself.'

'Hideo seemed to calm you down.'

'He was wonderful. I didn't dare tell him what was wrong because I didn't want to spread alarm but he somehow cheered me up. Hideo made me want to go on.'

'To good effect. You were in excellent form today.'

'That was before we drove back to the city, Alan.' I felt a shudder pass through her. 'Those were not idle threats I heard. A van tried to ram us and tip our car over the edge of the expressway. It was touch and go, honestly. We escaped by the skin of our teeth.'

'Could you see who was in the van?'

'Two men wearing stocking masks.'

'Did you get its number?'

'We had no time. There was just me and Keiko in the car. I was driving. The van came out of nowhere and charged into us. It disappeared in traffic before we knew what was happening. It was terrifying.'

'Did you report the incident to the police?'

'Straight away. They took down full details and said they'd be passed on to Superintendent Ushiba. Meanwhile, they advised, we had to be extra careful.'

'Didn't they offer you any kind of protection?'

'They promised to have a patrol car outside my hotel.'

'That's a great help!'

'I was too scared even to go back there,' she said. 'So I dropped Keiko off at her apartment then drove around to the lab to leave the equipment. It was the first time all day that I felt really safe because they have a proper security staff there so I hung about for a couple of hours. Then I rang here and discovered you'd gone out. I called a taxi, came over and waited outside your room. I'd been there about half an hour when you rolled up.'

She nuzzled into me for an affectionate squeeze.

'How does the idea of another brandy sound?' I said.

'Wonderful.'

'I'll join you.'

I poured two glasses then sat beside her again. Chiyo Takumi was a very self-possessed young woman who had been all over the world and had doubtless had to cope with a wide variety of difficult situations. Tough, experienced and proud of her independence, she would not be easily jangled. To find her in such a state suggested that there might be rather more to her story than had so far emerged so I concentrated on winning her confidence and making her relax. I let her go through it all again a couple of times before I told her about my own warnings. Chiyo was horrified to hear about my brush with Crew Cut and my Japanese massage, and she was amazed that I had not been deterred by either. At the same time, however, she disagreed with my overall analysis.

'You can't blame everything on Fumio,' she said.

'Why not?'

'He might threaten you because that's his jealousy coming out but he had no reason to lean so heavily on me. I mean, what's the point?'

'We can't make the video without a director.'

'I can be replaced,' she argued. 'You can't. The only sure way to stop an Alan Saxon video is to get rid of Alan Saxon. *You're* the main target.'

'So who tried to kill you?'

'Not Fumio. I'm certain of it.'

'Who else?'

'The person who killed Shohei.'

She blurted out the words then reeled from their impact, throwing down the second glass of brandy to steady herself as she weighed up their implications. As film director working on a cherished project, Chiyo Takumi was supremely impressive but, as a woman in real distress, she was vastly more interesting. I began to see weaknesses I had never suspected and sensitive areas I had never imagined. Sipping my own brandy, I tried to marry up the two opposing sides of my unexpected guest.

'How did you get involved in this project?' I said.

'By invitation.'

'But why you?'

'I like golf.'

'So do sixteen million other people in Japan.'

'They don't all have my track record as a director.'

'Did Shohei pick you out himself?'

'I was head-hunted.'

'By whom?'

'One of his underlings.'

'Didn't you find this video rather small beer?'

'What do you mean?'

'Well, Hideo was telling me about some of the other things you've directed. Real films with sizeable budgets. Wasn't this job a bit of a come-down?'

'You're joking!' she said. 'It pays well, it brought me back to Japan and it gave me a chance in a lifetime to work with you. I happen to be an Alan Saxon fan.'

'There's not many of us left.'

'We'd better stick together then.'

Sharing a laugh, we clinked our glasses then tasted some more brandy. Chiyo had shed much of her apprehension now and colour had returned to her face, renewing its beauty and bringing out its character. I realised with a light shock that we had never actually been alone together before and the experience was drawing me closer to her by the second. She read my mind then searched my eyes for a long time before coming to a conclusion.

'Can I stay?' she asked.

'Of course.'

'I don't mean...'

'No, that's okay,' I said quickly. 'You take the bed and I'll have the sofa.' 'But I want you with me.'

'Oh.'

'I need someone to cuddle, that's all.'

'Suits me.'

'You don't mind?'

'I'm very flattered.'

'It's because I trust you.'

'The bathroom is all yours...'

Fifteen minutes later, we were curled up together in the darkness. I wore pyjama trousers while Chiyo wore the top. It was not how I'd planned to spend the night but I was not complaining. She was soft, warm and suddenly fragile. It brought me even closer to her and I began to pick up new vibrations. It was almost as if Chiyo were putting me on trial to see if I justified her trust and I wondered what lay behind the experiment. An hour or more of gentle chat went by before I found out.

'How did you learn to play golf?' I said.

'When I was a teenager.'

'But who encouraged you? The majority of men in Japan never enjoy the luxury of playing on a proper golf course and it's probably worse for women.'

'Much worse.'

'So what makes you so different?'

'I played a lot of my golf abroad.'

'You must have learned the game here in Japan.'

'I did.'

'With someone paying those exorbitant green fees.'

'Yes.'

'Was it your father?'

'Oh, no.'

'Who, then?'

She scrunched herself up into a ball and pushed in against me. I held her tight and stroked her hair gently for several minutes. Her voice came out from under the sheets.

'I had a sponsor.'

'For your golfing lessons?'

'And for my career.'

'I thought you went to a film school in America.'

'Thanks to my guardian angel.'

'And who was that?'

I got my answer in the most unlikely way. She began to whimper, then sob, then weep so copiously that the tears ran down my bare chest. Her whole body was soon heaving as she gave full vent to her grief. Chiyo Takumi was an explanation in herself now. I understood why she had been selected to make the video and why completing it was such a sacred duty to her. I also realised why she had been so muted during the party at the Ogino household and so distraught by the tragedy that ensued. Her love of golf and her talent for film-making had both been developed with great care by a rich and sympathetic older man. She was the most closely guarded secret of the secretive Shohei Ogino.

'People only saw the worst,' she whispered. 'They only saw the callous businessman who drove everyone along with a crack of the whip. They only saw the tyrant who dominated his family. But Shohei was not like that at all. He was kind and considerate and full of tenderness. He really cared. Who could want to kill a man like that? He was wonderful.'

'How long did you know him?' I said.

'Years and years. It started when I was sixteen…'

Chiyo Takumi talked without embarrassment about a love which had shaped her entire adult life. In a country which set so much store by marriage, she had given up her own chances in order to become the mistress of a middle-aged man. At face value, it seemed a foolish and reprehensible thing to do but her account of the relationship soon swept away all trace of my disapproval. The picture of Shohei Ogino which now emerged was totally at variance with all the others I had grown so used to seeing. A staid family man turned out to have flights of romantic folly. An austere tycoon was revealed as a man of true compassion. The father who had been so proprietorial about his own daughter had contrived a long-term affair with someone of almost exactly the same age. Chiyo was far more than just a repository for his sexual fantasies. She was the child-bride of someone who had sustained a deep and lasting love for her over a period of more than a decade. When she embarked on her story, I was faintly revolted by the very idea of such a liaison with all its undertones of exploitation and perversion. By the time she had finished, I came to admire and envy what they had shared between them, marvelling at the degree of secrecy and discretion that was involved and genuinely touched by the insight I'd been permitted.

Without her mentor, lover and father-figure, Chiyo had been cut adrift and was floating aimlessly.

'Who killed him?' she said. 'Who killed him?'

She was still asking the question as she fell asleep.

◇◇◇

I awoke next morning to find my hands enmeshed in the pyjama jacket, but it now lacked its former occupant. My first thought was that it had all been some kind of hallucination brought on by deep-seated desires hidden away in my psyche, but Chiyo's special fragrance still lingered unmistakeably. Fearing that she had left in the night, I got up at once to check then heard the reassuring sound of the bath being filled. I had to bang hard on the door before she heard me.

'Yes?' she called.

'Good morning!'

'Hi, Alan.'

'Are you hungry?'

'Famished.'

'What would you like for breakfast?'

'Everything.'

'Leave it to me.'

I rang Room Service and ordered two full breakfasts then I sat back on the bed and reflected on all that I had learned since I climbed into it with her. Chiyo Takumi was quite extraordinary. She was a high-achiever whose ambitions had been fuelled by a man of immense vision who did all he could to advance her career even though it took her away from him. Golf had first bonded them together and he had taken as much pleasure in developing her playing skills as he had in turning Fumio into a brilliant professional. The instructional video had not just been a way of luring me to Japan. It had been the perfect cover for Chiyo's return to her native city. To Shohei Ogino, the project was, in every sense, a labour of love.

Chiyo's midnight confession had given me a whole new perspective on the Ogino family. It had also provided the murderer of Shohei with a motive that I had never even considered before. Jealousy might easily have constructed the exploding cigar box. Masako would not have been the first wife moved to homicidal rage by the discovery of her husband's adultery and it was well inside the bounds of possibility that Chiyo had an ardent admirer who realised that the only way to get close to her was to eliminate her long-standing lover. There was now a third contender for the killing of Shohei Ogino, someone who could find the truth about him too much to bear if it had finally come to light. Mitsu very definitely became a suspect. In view of the brutal way her father had ended her affair with Sam Limsong, she had every right to feel vengeful and that feeling would have been greatly intensified. It was vital that I talked to Mitsu at the earliest opportunity.

Breakfast arrived on a trolley to interrupt my cogitations and I broke off to admit the waiter, then send him on his way with a tip. A tap on the bathroom door got an instant answer this time.

'Yes?' said Chiyo.

'Breakfast is served.'

'Be out in a few minutes.'

'No hurry.'

It gave me ample time to make an important telephone call. Picking up my address book from the bedside table, I found the number I wanted and dialled. A maid answered in Japanese and it took me a few moments to get my message through and to train her into saying something that actually resembled my name. The brusque voice of Mitsu Ogino then came on the line.

'What do you want?'

'I need to see you again.'

'That won't be possible, I'm afraid.'

'Why not?'

'Because we've said all we need to each other.'

'I don't agree.'

'Goodbye, Alan.'

'Neither does Sam Limsong.'

She recoiled. 'What are you talking about?'

'An overnight flight I took to Bangkok. Sam and I only had a short time together but it was very enlightening. It explained why someone fitted an Ogino bugging device inside my golf bag. And why you have every right to loathe your father as much as you do.'

'It's...not a good idea to meet,' she faltered.

'Too bad. Let's make it this evening, shall we?'

'Alan...'

'I get back here about six-thirty,' I said. 'You choose the time and place then leave me a message in Reception. I'll lurk under any cherry tree you decide on.'

I could hear her thinking it through at the other end of the line. More pressure was obviously needed.

'Sam was very explicit. He told me everything.'

'I don't believe you.'

'He explained how the pair of you got it together when you were in the States. And how your father found out. He also told me how...'

'That's enough,' she snapped.

'It still rankles with Sam as well.'

'Don't keep on about it.'

'Then meet me tonight. When you rang me, I came running straight away. Now it's my turn. Be seeing you. Okay?'

'Okay,' she consented.

'Thanks.'

I hung up the receiver then found myself a kimono to slip over my naked torso. Chiyo and I had got very close during the night but I knew that those moments of intimacy were only temporary and this was confirmed when she came out of the bathroom a couple of minutes later. Dressed in denim once more, she had the patina of professionalism firmly back in place and she did not want to be reminded of what had happened between us. Over breakfast, I saw, we would talk about nothing except golf. All the burning questions that I was dying to ask her, therefore, had to be subsumed into one.

'How do you like your coffee?'

◇◇◇

Takeshi Ogino was as good as his word. When the limousine came to pick us up from the hotel, it had a woman at the driving wheel. Half an hour beforehand, Chiyo had tactfully departed and taken a taxi back to the laboratory where she arranged to be picked up by her cameramen. After the incident on the previous day, she did not wish to travel in her own car again. Clive Phelps and I got into the back of the limousine and set off. Since we'd had no word from Hideo Nakane, we assumed that he was making his own way to the Wada International Country Club. Bright sunshine favoured our enterprise once again and turned the early morning traffic jam on the expressway into a long, gleaming serpent that was coiling itself around Tokyo.

There was no point in even trying to confide in Clive. He would never understand. To share a bed with a beautiful woman and settle for companionship was an experience way outside his cosmology. Since the woman in question was Chiyo Takumi, it would have been even more impossible to convince him that nothing more took place in the darkness than cuddle and confessional. The added complication of Clive's own interest in her reinforced my decision to keep him blissfully ignorant. What I did do—by prior agreement with Chiyo herself—was to tell him about the van which had tried to ram her car. He was justifiably angry.

'That's appalling!' he yelled.

'I know.'

'What happened to the safest capital city in the world? Everything's suddenly gone haywire here. Smoke a cigar and they blow you up. Drive on the expressway and they try to tip you off. Has Chiyo been on to the Laughing Policeman?'

'Ushiba will have got all the details by now.'

'Well, I hope he pulls his finger out and takes some action. We can't have our Director ambushed by thugs. She needs a couple of coppers to ride shotgun.'

'She's with her camera crew this morning.'

'What good are they in an emergency?' he said. 'We want someone who can prevent an attack, not film the bloody thing while it's happening.'

'I'm sure Ushiba will do something.'

'I'm not. All the bugger's done so far is to give us his impersonation of the Cheshire Cat. Hell's Bells! Ogino is murdered and the good Superintendent flashes his wall-to-wall grin. What did he do when they dropped the atom bomb on Nagasaki—have a fit of the giggles?'

'Ushiba is a very able man,' I conceded.

'Let him prove it. If he's such a shrewd cookie, let him make a few arrests. Starting with those bastards who tried to knock poor Chiyo off the road.'

'He has to find them first.'

'Then he can chuckle all over them.'

Clive railed on for a long time about the shortcomings of the police. The motorised assault on Chiyo had really distressed him because it was an attempt to sabotage the project which had brought us both to Japan and in which he had an emotional as well as a professional investment. He was also discovering just how fond he was of Chiyo herself.

'What an ordeal for her!'

'She sounded rattled over the phone,' I said.

'Rattled! I'd be fucking well gibbering!'

'Me, too.'

'Chiyo needs to be comforted.'

'I think she'd rather just get on with the job.'

'She's a woman, Saxon. She needs a shoulder to cry on.'

'That's not my reading of the situation.'

'What do you know about it?'

He launched himself into another tirade against police incompetence and I stopped listening. While Clive was still protesting about what had occurred the previous day, I was trying to work out who had ordered it. My dismissal of Fumio Ogino from the list of suspects had been too hasty. Chiyo's testimony had provided the youngest of the three brothers with a very real motive to get rid of her. If he had found out about his father's involvement with her, he would be both disgusted and incensed, horrified that she was in a position to bring such dishonour on his family and outraged that her own golfing abilities had been nurtured alongside his own. In disposing of her, he would be removing a hate-figure from his warped little world at the same time as he was stopping work on the video. Fumio had already proved that he was no gentleman. He was more than capable of ordering the murder of two defenceless young ladies in a car.

Clive's tempest blew itself out and left him in melancholy vein. With a wistful eye on the shining black hair of our chauffeuse, he heaved a deep sigh.

'I think I'm losing my touch.'

'With what?'

'Women. I've been in this damn city for ten days or more now and I still haven't scored. It's humiliating. I like to spread my love around.'

'Save it for your wife.'

'I can't wait *that* long!'

'Address your mind to higher things.'

'There *is* no higher thing then sex.'

'What about golf?'

'It's just another version of it.'

'Since when?'

'Since the game was first invented,' he said irritably. 'Come on, Saxon. We're all boys together here. Face the truth. Golf is phallocentric. I mean, what's the object of the exercise?'

'To win.'

'To propel a small white ball from the end of a stiff shaft into a beckoning hole. It's sex by numbers. Have you forgotten what you said the other day? About getting a hard-on when you're standing on the green?'

'It was a figure of speech, Clive.'

'An accurate one. Take your average golfer, crouched over a putt that's twelve inches from the hole. He *knows* that he's on a cert so what does he do? He gives that telltale little smirk.'

'A celebration of success.'

'The smile before the dick goes in.'

'Don't you think you're labouring the point?'

'Not at all. Golf is fornication in public.' He heard himself and laughed. 'Take no notice of me. I'm just feeling horny and frustrated. Maybe I should take up basket-weaving or something. As a form of sublimation.' He laughed again. 'Waste of time. I'd probably get so frantic, I'd end up fucking the basket.'

'What's on the agenda for today?'

'First off, I must console Chiyo.'

'She'll want to submerge herself in her work,' I said. 'Except that you'd probably call that work voyeurism.'

'A film camera is nothing but a keyhole.'

'And what is the butler going to see through it today?'

'Approach spots to the green.'

'That sounds harmless enough.'

'Not really. It's a case of getting up.'

My turn to sigh. 'Thank you, Clive. Let's talk about something else, shall we? When you're in one of these cynical moods, there's no way that I can cheer you up.'

'Yes, there is.'

'How?'

'Tell me the Japanese for "Are you free tonight?"'

'Why?'

'So that I can try it out on Madame Butterfly here,' he said, indicating our driver. 'I tell you, Saxon, I'm so bloody desperate, I'll take *anyone*. Apart from you.'

I was glad that I didn't tell him about Chiyo.

◇◇◇

As we pulled into the car park at the Wada International Country Club, a white Nissan rolled in behind us and stopped a short distance away. The two men in the vehicle made no attempt to get out. They watched quietly as Clive and I got my golf bag from the boot and headed towards the clubhouse. Hideo Nakane came hurrying towards us with controlled anxiety. There was a piece of sticking plaster above one eyebrow on the diagonal and a bruise on his cheekbone.

'What happened to you?' asked Clive.

'I had a visitor this morning,' said Hideo.

'Strong-arm stuff?'

'He told me not to come here any more.'

'My God, they're trying to frighten everyone off. It'll be my turn next.'

'All I got was a slight roughing up,' said Hideo, touching his cheek gingerly. 'Chiyo had far worse last night. Have you heard?'

'She rang me,' I said. 'Very alarming.'

'Diabolical!' added Clive. 'What's going on here? We try to make a harmless little video and someone sets an assassination squad on to us. We need protection.'

'You've got it now,' said Hideo, nodding towards the white Nissan. 'They trailed you from the hotel.'

'Did Ushiba send them?' I wondered.

'Takeshi. Private security. Another car acted as a bodyguard for Chiyo as well. They're going to stay close all the time from now on.'

'That's a relief!' said Clive.

As we strolled towards the clubhouse, the occupants of the Nissan got out and followed at a leisurely pace. Chiyo was waiting with her crew. She waved aside all enquiries about the attack and insisted that we got on with the task in hand as soon as possible. When I'd changed in the locker room, we went straight out to tackle the day's schedule. Chiyo was even more exuberant than usual, leaping about and urging us on, communicating her enthusiasm with infectious glee. It was almost as if she were giving a performance for the benefit of her attackers, reaffirming her faith in the project and offering them a calculated act of defiance. She was also paying homage to Shohei Ogino. It would take more than a couple of thugs in a van to prevent her from doing that.

After two excellent, if attenuated, days of filming, we hit one of those patches where everything went wrong. The cameraman made mistakes, we had unforeseen technical problems and drifting cloud caused variation of light, but the worst offender was myself. Not only did I stumble and stutter through the script, I fared little better when I let my golf clubs do the talking for me. I simply could not find my rhythm and shot after shot went astray. After a particularly bad slice which sent my ball irretrievably into a small copse, I stamped my foot and glowered darkly. Clive Phelps sidled up to me with a sly grin.

'See? I told you. Golf is just like sex.'

'This is not the smile before the dick goes in.'

'No, but you've got a face like a faked orgasm.'

I made strenuous efforts to improve after that.

We did better after lunch and clawed back some of the time that had been squandered but it was still one of our less successful days. Chiyo, however, refused to be abashed by it all and she gave us a pep talk as we dispersed. I heard what she said but my eye was distracted by something that appeared on the clubhouse steps. Over her shoulder, I saw a group of a dozen or so business-men who were watching us with great interest. One of them did not like the fact that I was looking at him and he slunk quickly away before I could work out what he was doing there. Given his known indifference to the game, the man's presence there was puzzling. It was also rather disturbing.

Yasayuki Ogino was a shadow on the grass.

◇◇◇

Her message was waiting for me at Reception when we returned and I opened the envelope at once. Clive Phelps was enraged when I told him that I had to go out again on my own that evening, convinced that it was to another assignation and that I would succeed where he had so far signally failed. There was a heated exchange in the lift but we parted amicably enough in the corridor when I told him that I would ask my mystery woman if she would be interested in meeting a golf writer from England. His drooping moustache bristled with new interest. A shave, a bath and a change of clothes revived me and I then consulted my map of Tokyo. The venue this time was an apart-ment in the Shibuya area.

Leaving the Imperial Hotel was a slow and methodical busi-ness because I feared I was still under surveillance. The security men who had guarded us at the golf course had certainly gone but there was always the chance that Akio Ushiba had placed someone on duty at my place of residence. In addition to those who were supposedly on my side, there was also Crew Cut and any unsavoury colleagues he might have. I'd openly ignored the warning from Fumio Ogino and he would want to exact revenge at some stage. Exercising the utmost care, therefore, I patrolled the corridors and skirted the lounge three times before slipping out into the night. A providential taxi whisked me away at speed. After five minutes glued to the rear window, I was certain that I was not being followed.

Shibuya is a hilly district towards the north of the city, known chiefly as a playground for the youth of Tokyo because of its proximity to several University campuses. I imagined that Mitsu

Ogino might have connections there from her own student days. It was a long drive and my wallet was bracing itself for frontal attack by the taxi meter. By the time we reached the station, I'd lost count of the number of trendy clothing stores, speciality shops, restaurants, bars and cinemas that we'd passed in the neon jungle. Koen Dori Street seemed to be one continuous stream of boutiques and fashion houses. The taxi finally dropped me outside one of them and I paid my bill with the required valour.

The apartment was down a narrow sidestreet that was filled with the aroma of a charcoal grill. I went in through a door and up some stairs before knocking. Mitsu's voice was cautious.

'Who is it?'

'Alan Saxon.'

'Are you sure you're alone?'

'Quite sure.'

'Come in.'

The door opened to admit me then closed immediately. I was in a small room with minimal furniture. It was lit by a table lamp which threw up a rather vivid light. Caught in its glare, Mitsu looked sickly and distraught. She told me that the apartment belonged to an old college friend of hers then she waved me to a seat. There was no preamble.

'What did Sam really tell you?' she said.

'That you and he became very close.'

'He promised to say nothing!'

'These were rather special circumstances.'

'You went all the way to Bangkok?'

'I played my hunch,' I said. 'Sam was being so evasive that I knew he was hiding something vital. I'd also worked out that the bugging device planted on me was really for his benefit. Any idea who could have put it in my bag?'

'Father.'

'Was he that keen to maintain a watch on Sam Limsong?'

'He despised him.' Mitsu rubbed the palms of her hands together then looked down at them before continuing. 'My father was not a nice man. You'll know how he found out about us and tore us apart. That wasn't enough for him. He was like a mad dog. Once he sank his teeth into someone, he never let go.'

'Why did he hate Sam so much?'

'Because of me. Japanese women are expected to be docile and to conceal any education they get. It's the only way to find what they call "a good husband". I'd already upset my father by my radical views and behaviour. He began to fear that nobody would marry me. My friendship with Sam Limsong was the final straw. It was symbolic. In getting involved with a Thai, I was cutting myself off from my own country and betraying some of its oldest traditions. I was turning my back on any hope of a Japanese husband.' She grimaced slightly. 'My father was furious.'

'What did he do to Sam?'

'Had him beaten up and tried to discredit him.'

'Bad publicity?'

'Father had many journalists in his pocket.'

'How did Sam react?'

'He was very brave but it got him down in the end. You have no idea how vicious a man like my father could be.'

'Tell me, Mitsu.'

She talked for several minutes and new crimes were laid at the feet of Shohei Ogino. Whatever his virtues as a lover to Chiyo Takumi, he was an unfeeling father who sought to impose his will from above. Mitsu talked of their frequent battles and of his attempts to limit her freedom. Going to America was the final escape from him and she had signalled her new-found liberty by having the affair with Sam Limsong. Its consequences could still rack her with guilt.

'I feel so sorry for him,' she said.

'He must have known the risks.'

'Sam loved me. That made it all much more painful.'

'Didn't *you* love him?'

'Not really.'

'Then why did you get involved with him?' She shook her head dismissively. 'Why, Mitsu? Were you using Sam?'

'No.'

'Were you waving him at your father deliberately?'

'Of course not.'

'Were you trying to get your own back?'

'It wasn't like that.'

'Then what was it like?'

'I can't tell you.'

'I'm not leaving until you do.'

She could see that I was serious. Having come so far, I was not going to back down without finding out everything that she could tell me. Mitsu Ogino was not only guilty because of the way that Sam Limsong had been victimised. There was another reason and I kept on at her until she weakened enough to let it seep out.

'There was someone else.'

'Another lover?'

'No, no,' she said. 'Someone I didn't like, someone who kept chasing me even after I begged him not to. He came to Boston to see me. It was dreadful. There was only one way that I could get rid of him.'

'By having an affair with someone else.'

She nodded. 'I feel so sorry for Sam. We had some good times together. And I did...sort of love him.'

'Only not enough,' I said harshly. 'If you'd stood by him, your father would never have dared to touch him. Sam was not only used to keep this other person at bay. When the going got tough, he was sacrificed to your father.'

'Don't say that!'

'It's the truth, isn't it?'

'Only partly.'

'Sam Limsong was expendable.'

'No!'

'He was set up.'

'NO!'

Her scream of protest was followed by a flood of tears that cut most of the resistance out of her and sent her into my arms.

I soothed her until she stopped crying then gave her my handkerchief to dab at her eyes. Mitsu Ogino was overwhelmed by
remorse and I sensed why.

'You *wanted* him to find out, didn't you?' I said.

'Yes...'

'You wanted to hurt your father and this was the best way of
doing it. His only daughter, turning her back on all his values
and jumping into bed with a foreigner. A Thai at that. It must've
wounded your father to the quick.'

'Not only him.'

'What?'

'Fumio, too,' she admitted.

'You wanted to strike back at him as well?'

'That's why it had to be Sam.'

There was defiance mixed in with her guilt, a proud boast
that she had achieved her aim even though it meant delivering up a victim to her family's anger. Sam Limsong had been
genuinely in love with her when he embarked on the affair but
Mitsu's commitment was only skin-deep. It was more important
to her to hit out at a father and brother whom she hated than
to protect a man who really cared for her. Beneath her softness
and sophistication, there was a calculating selfishness that was
quite repulsive. I recalled the scene at Bangkok Airport. Sam
Limsong would be far better off with the doting Somjai.

'Where does Ushuba fit into all this?' I said.

'He advised my father.'

'The private detective?'

'One of his contacts.'

'Is that the sort of work Ushiba did for your father?'

'Yes. He arranges things.'

I wondered if the smiling Superintendent knew about
Shohei's dark secret. I was now certain that Mitsu did not. She
could generate enough hatred of her father without a glimmer
of knowledge about Chiyo Takumi. It was best kept that way.
Enough damage had already been caused.

'Who was the other man?' I said. 'The one who pursued you to Boston? Is he still around?'

'That was all over a year ago.'

'What was his name?'

'Please, Alan,' she said, returning my handkerchief. 'I've told you more than I should have. There's nothing else, I swear. Let me alone now.'

'I just want to ask one thing...'

But there was no time even to put my question. The telephone rang and she started back. Controlling her fear, she picked up the receiver and spoke into it in Japanese. The message she got made her eyes widen with horror and she looked across at me.

'It's Fumio. He knows you're here.'

'How?'

'Get out, Alan.'

'What did he say?'

'Just get out while you can.'

Self-preservation made me abandon any further discussion. I followed her to the rear of the apartment and into a small kitchen. The window gave out on to a fire escape that zigzagged down the side of the building. I needed no second invitation. Lifting the window, I peered out to establish that nobody was about then eased myself slowly through. The steel steps led down to a tiny courtyard between the apartment block and the neighbouring buildings. I descended as swiftly and silently as I could until I reached the ground, then dodged down an alley that seemed to lead back to the main street. When I reached the corner, I inched my head around it but I saw almost nothing.

Before I could take stock of my situation, something thin and hot was flicked around my neck from behind and a knee went into the small of my back. It was agonising. As the cord tightened, I brought up both hands to try to loosen it but its grip was inexorable. I was being strangled to death. Fighting to pull forward, I was dragged steadily backwards by the power of my assailant and my eyes became completely blurred. It was not a warning this time that galvanised me into action. I did the only thing that I could think of, using my attacker's strength against him by suddenly hurling myself backwards with full force, knocking him hard against a stone wall and winding him sufficiently to make him let go of his lethal cord. As I gulped in air, I rubbed at the burning weal on my neck, relieved that my head was still attached to my body.

Gathering my strength, I swung round to confront what I felt sure would be Crew Cut but a much slighter figure was facing me. He was an eerie sight. Wearing a black stocking mask, dark trousers and polo-neck sweater, he plucked a knife from a sheath on his belt and came back at me. Niceties went by the board. This was raw survival. As he circled me and tried a few passes with the knife, I reacted instinctively and lashed out with a large foot at the end of a very long leg. He took the blow on his shin and grunted in pain. My next kick caught him firmly in the crotch and made him double up for a second before straightening angrily to hurl the knife at me with vicious force. It missed by inches as I ducked beneath it, bouncing off the wall to clatter to the ground.

My adversary was not done yet. Landing a kick of his own on my thigh, he swung a murderous fist that clipped my jaw and had me reeling. He moved in for the kill when the sound of running feet deterred him. Two figures were sprinting down the alley towards us. My attacker threw a farewell punch at me and gave me one tiny flashing clue to his identity. The gold ring on the little finger of his left hand sparkled momentarily in the light then grazed my cheek as I moved my head to avoid the punch. With the others closing in, the masked figure took to his heels and vanished into the main thoroughfare.

Turning to face the two newcomers, I braced myself for further violence but they had come to help. One of them steadied me and checked for injury while his companion took up the pursuit. In spite of my fear, pain and confusion, I got a small thrill of pleasure. I could not remember who wore that ring on his little finger but it had flashed at me like that once before. I knew the man.

Chapter Eleven

Superintendent Akio Ushiba had stopped laughing. As he sat behind the desk in his office, his face was serious and his eyebrows formed a chevron of concern. Perched on a seat opposite him, I sipped gratefully at the cup of tea I had been given and resolved to tell him as little as possible. My second conversation with Mitsu Ogino had exploded the myth of the friendly policeman. Ushiba's role in her family affairs was highly ambiguous. Bereft of his grin, he had the faintly sinister air of a cut-price Buddha. It was quite impossible to tell which side he was really on—except that it was very definitely not mine.

A jocular tone tried to restore his credibility.

'You give my men such a hard time, Alan,' he said.

'Do I?'

'They could not keep up with you last night. How can they protect you if you give them the slip?'

'I wasn't sure they were offering protection.'

'What else?'

'Invigilation.'

He dredged up a chuckle but it carried no conviction.

'I thought you needed help.'

'Yes—against the police.'

'My men saved you in that alley.'

'That's a moot point,' I said. 'They came too late and ran too slow. I needed them when I was being throttled. I wanted them there when a knife was being brandished at me.'

'You sneaked off without telling them.'

'What do they require—a telegram?'

He clicked his tongue. 'Have you never heard of the idea of co-operating with law-enforcement officers?'

'My father rammed it down my throat every day.'

'Why make things so difficult for yourself?'

'Force of habit, Superintendent.'

'You could have been killed in that alley.'

'I know. I was there.'

The police had not captured my assailant. He had fled into the back-streets of Shibuya and shaken off his pursuer. I had been brought back to Ushiba's office in a squad car so that he could probe for information. It was not the kind of situation that brings out the amenable side of my nature.

'Why did you meet up with Mitsu Ogino?' he asked.

'Is that what I did?'

'Don't play games, Alan. She was seen leaving the apartment that you visited.'

'Then why not ask her?'

'I'm asking *you*.'

'Didn't you use a bugging device this time?'

Ushiba glowered. One hand played with the Rolex watch on the other wrist as he sat back in his chair to appraise me with an amalgam of hostility and grudging admiration.

'I thought we were friends, Alan.'

'Not inside this office.'

'I hoped we understood each other.'

'A mistake in the translation.'

'Stop trying to do our job for us.'

'Someone has to, Superintendent.'

'We've been working around the clock to solve this murder,' he said with asperity. 'Our investigations have taken us all over Japan as well as abroad. An enormous amount of data and hard evidence has been collected. We may have our faults, Alan, but we're not lazy.'

'Just misdirected.'

'What do you mean?'

'Well, why waste manpower trailing innocent people like me when you could be concentrating on the real suspects?'

'Such as?'

'The family, for a start.'

'Be careful, Alan...'

'That cigar box was planted in Shohei's study by someone with ready access to the house. That puts three names at the very top of the list.'

'Not in my opinion.'

'Takeshi. Yasayuki. Fumio.'

'They are not involved.'

'One of them has to be, Superintendent.'

'I know the family a lot better than you.'

'Yes,' I retorted. 'You've been on the Ogino payroll.'

Smarting under the insult, he stood to his feet and glared across at me, holding back the reply he was tempted to make. His anger was quickly controlled and smothered under a quiet chuckle. He nodded as if conceding a point to me.

'So that is why you went to Bangkok.'

'It was a fruitful visit.'

'What did Sam Limsong tell you?'

'Enough.'

'I felt sorry for him. Mitsu was to blame. What happened between them was very sad.'

'You got something out of it.'

'The satisfaction of helping an old friend. That is all, I fear. Shohei never paid me a single yen.' He strolled across to me. 'Sorry to disappoint you, Alan. My only income is from the Tokyo Metropolitan Police.' He stood over me. 'I earn it legally and honourably.'

'How well did you know Shohei Ogino?'

'As well as he let me.'

'Could he have had any dark secrets?'

'Lots of them,' he said with a grin. 'Which of us doesn't? We have uncovered a few of them already.'

'Any real scandal?'

'Unfortunately, no. He was far too conventional.'

I was relieved. Chiyo Takumi had eluded the gaze of this shrewd professional. It spoke volumes for the discretion that Shohei Ogino must have exercised and confirmed just how much the relationship must have meant to both of them. There was no point in betraying the dead man now and I got another quiet surge of pleasure at the thought of being in possession of privileged information. It was one item in my own private collection. The bugging device in Bangkok. Threats from Fumio. A near-fatal Japanese massage. A secret love affair. A gold ring worn on the little finger of the left hand. Superintendent Akio Ushiba and his murder squad detectives knew about none of these things. All I had to do was to connect them together in some way.

'It was not one of the sons,' said Ushiba.

'How can you be so sure?'

'They are Japanese. They respected their father.'

'He controlled all three of them like puppets.'

'Shohei was a strong-willed man.'

'His children all hated him as a result.'

'It makes no difference. He was their father.'

'I don't follow.'

'*Fishin, kaminari, kaji, oyaji...*'

'Another proverb?'

'Of course. Earthquakes, thunderbolts, fires, fathers.' He went back behind his desk and wagged a finger. 'Fear those greater than yourself.'

I saw his argument. Takeshi, Yasayuki and Fumio might each have good reason to want their father dead but they were too afraid to kill him themselves. In their codex, a father was indeed like a major catastrophe and I found an affinity with them. Earthquakes, thunderbolts, fires, fathers. Inspector Tom Saxon fitted neatly into the concept and I saw the disasters in ascending order of magnitude. The three sons of Shohei Ogino and I were poles apart in everything but we had common cause on this. Fathers who policed our lives from above took on the quality of natural phenomena. Childhood consisted in running before the storm.

Finishing my tea, I got up to replace the cup on the edge of the desk and to ask a special favour.

'Could you call your trusty men off, please?'

'No bodyguards?'

'I'd rather take my own chances.'

'That man in the alleyway could strike again.'

'I won't talk to any strange men.'

Ushiba chuckled then nodded his agreement. With an arm around my shoulder, he led me across to the door.

'Do you know *why* I gave you police protection?'

'Because I love it so much!'

'No, Alan. Because you are the focus.'

'Of what?'

'This murder investigation,' he said. 'Everything comes back to the game of golf. Does the name of Doki Securities mean anything to you?'

'No. Should it?'

'One of our biggest finance companies.'

'Where do they fit into the picture?'

'As the future owners of Packwood Heath Golf Course.'

I was astounded. 'They've bought it?'

'Not yet but it's very much on the cards. I took the trouble to ring our colleagues at New Scotland Yard and they made some enquiries. It seems that Shohei had been stalking Packwood Heath for two years and he was on the point of signing the contract with the course management. Then a new bidder came out of the blue.'

'Doki Securities.'

'Shohei must have been livid. This was something he handled personally and in strict secrecy. After nursing the negotiations along for two years, he then has someone else trying to steal the course from under his nose.'

'How did this other company know about Packwood Heath?'

'That's what we're trying to find out.'

'Does this Doki Securities have enough financial muscle to take on Shohei Electrical?'

'More than enough but it's no longer a fight between two giants. One of them has conveniently retired. Needless to say, we're pressing Doki all we can but they're giving very little away. And they've done nothing illegal.'

'Unless they had their rival eliminated.'

'It's a possibility we have to look at,' he said as he opened the door for me. 'But you catch my drift? A golf course in England and an instructional video in Tokyo. Those are crucial elements in Shohei's death. That is where Alan Saxon comes in.'

'As a link between the two?'

'Exactly. It is the main reason why you have been kept here to continue your filming.'

'Takeshi wants to honour his father's contract.'

'He is also following my advice. If you stay here and work on that video, the killer may be lured out of hiding. Now do you see why you have police cover, Alan? He gave the broadest grin yet. 'You're the bait on the hook.'

◇ ◇ ◇

Shocked by Ushiba's cheery revelation and still shaken by events in an alleyway in Shibuya, I left police headquarters with mixed feelings. Nominally free of any protection, I felt for the first time that I really needed it and yet the very notion caused a deep psychic wound to reopen. It was quite bewildering. I decided on balance that I was far better off without any of Ushiba's men tailing me. My father was company enough. I carried my own policeman everywhere.

Released from official cover, I would be an even more inviting target and this made me ultra-cautious. My first task, I decided, must be to shake off pursuit of any kind and Tokyo Station suggested itself. I took a taxi there then darted around its cavernous interior, hiding in corners or lurking behind banks of left-luggage lockers to make sure that nobody was after me. It was half an hour before I abandoned my solo game of hide-and-seek. A second taxi took me across to the New Otani Hotel in Chiyoda-ku. If you are in a mood for heady excess, it implores a visit.

The hotel is set in a ten-acre traditional Japanese garden that is reputedly four hundred years old. In stark contrast, the buildings that mushroom out of it are palaces of modernity. With over two thousand rooms and superb facilities, the New Otani has everything. To someone who spends most of his domestic life in a motor caravan, it was like stepping into a kind of futuristic cathedral. I used a courtesy phone to ring Chiyo Takumi but she was not in her room. When I had her paged, she turned up in one of the bars. Surprised but pleased to see me, she led me across to a quiet table in a corner and ordered a fresh bottle of white wine.

'You've just missed Hideo,' she said.

'What was he doing here?'

'Helping me with tomorrow's schedule. He's been like a right arm to me and it's so good to have company when you're feeling a bit jittery.'

'There's nothing to worry about,' I reassured.

'Alan, we're in the firing line.'

'Just keep your wits about you.'

'Aren't you scared?'

'Intermittently.'

The wine arrived to restore us and we toasted the success of the video, both hoping that we would be allowed to complete it. Chiyo looked and sounded like a hard-edged career woman but she still felt highly insecure about what had happened. Though we had a tacit agreement not to talk about her past again, I had no option.

'We must speak about Shohei,' I said.

'That's all over, Alan.'

'I'm afraid not.'

'There's nothing more to say.'

'Wait until you hear what Ushiba told me.'

I gave her a diluted version of it all, explaining the crucial role of the golf video while trying to minimise the personal danger to us. She was at once fascinated and terrified, eager to learn anything about the activities of her former lover yet distressed by the implications of what she was hearing. Evidently, she knew nothing at all about the negotiations for the purchase of Packwood Heath and I was amazed once more by the ability of Shohei Ogino to maintain such impenetrable levels of secrecy. It was as if he put his whole life into a series of safe-deposit boxes, each of them containing people and projects that were separate from all the others. I tapped on the door of Chiyo's box.

'Did he ever mention Doki Securities to you?'

'No.'

'Not even a casual reference?'

'He simply never talked business.'

'What about family matters?'

'Strictly forbidden.'

'He never talked about his wife?'

Chiyo bristled. 'I'd have been very annoyed if he had.'

'What about his daughter?'

'Mitsu never came up either. For obvious reasons.'

I saw what she meant. No man would be tactless enough to discuss a daughter who was roughly the same age as the young woman with whom he was having an affair. The box that Chiyo shared with Shohei Ogino had love, luxury and warmth in it. Business and family were outlawed. I thanked her for her help and let her close the door again before throwing away the key. Nobody else would ever know what was inside now.

We chatted about the day's shooting and the plans for the next day then I took my leave. Chiyo walked me to the main doors then threw me an interesting titbit.

'There'll be three of you in the car tomorrow?'

'Does Hideo want another lift?'

'No, but I suspect that Keiko will.'

'She usually travels with you.'

'Not when she stays at the Imperial Hotel.'

I raised a quizzical eyebrow. 'Clive?'

'He talked her into it.'

'Good luck to both of them, I say!'

'So do I, Alan. It lets me out.'

It would also make Clive Phelps more cheerful. After recurring failures that sapped his spirit, he had finally found someone. Keiko would lift his gloom admirably.

◇◇◇

To ensure that I was not being followed, I went through an elaborate pantomime with taxis. The first took me to the Shimbashi Hotel which I left instantly by the rear exit. The second dropped me back at Tokyo Station where I utilised favourite hiding places as before, then the third took me on the short journey to the Imperial Hotel. When I had taken all the extra precautions I could devise, I came to the firm conclusion that I was safe. Ushiba's men had definitely been withdrawn and there was no whiff of any lurking enemies at any stage of my travels since leaving police headquarters. Clive Phelps was at last in bed with a pliable young woman and all was right with the world.

As I made the final tour of the ground floor, my mind was fixed on the gold ring. Many of the men with whom I'd had dealings in Tokyo wore rings of some kind. Akio Ushiba had three to complement the Rolex, Takeshi had two, Yasayuki and Shohei had one apiece. Both of the cameramen wore wedding rings. There were dozens more that I'd glimpsed during my stay but it was an item I took little notice of as a rule because of the need to discard my own wedding ring when Rosemary and I divorced. What made the gold ring in the alleyway so unusual was the fact that it was so small and yet reflected so much light. It was also shaped like a miniature diamond. I knew that I'd seen it once before but could not call up the memory from a tired brain.

Sleep was now the priority. Even before the exertions of an evening in Shibuya, I was feeling jaded and weary. A herbal bath and a relatively early night were called for and I made my way upstairs on foot. The corridor was long, wide and well-lit.

Satisfied there was nobody lying in ambush, I opened the door of my room and stepped quickly inside. I slammed home the bolt and inserted the safety chain before coming into the middle of the room, only to find that I had just cut off my escape. An imposing, bull-necked figure stepped out from an alcove to confront me with eyes ablaze. Crew Cut was back. When I swung back to the door, I realised that I could never unlock it in time. The bathroom was the only option but that was a false friend. As I lunged towards it, a second Crew Cut emerged with arms akimbo. I was caught between the two of them with nowhere else to go. They made an ominous pair, each a replica of the other, matching cigar boxes that would both explode to order.

I got in a few punches to face and midriff before burly arms imprisoned me. One punch in the solar plexus was enough to knock a lot of the resistance out of me.

'Can't Fumio do his own dirty trick?' I gasped.

'You, quiet,' ordered Crew Cut One.

'He can't beat me on a golf course so he sends you two goons around here. That's a coward's way out.'

'You warned. Ask for trouble.'

'Give him a message from me. He's a lousy golfer.'

'Shut mouth.'

'Fumio Ogino will never make it among the men!'

My shout of defiance earned a slap across the face that made my head ring but it also saved me from any additional punishment. Fumio himself stepped out of the bathroom.

'Stop!' he snapped.

The twin Crew Cuts obeyed with ugly reluctance. They were unhappy about being robbed of their regular night-time entertainment. I was clearly their punch bag.

'You no good golfer,' said Fumio with contempt.

'I agree,' I said, 'but that still puts me way ahead of you. Let's face it. You're still a floundering amateur.'

'A pro! A pro! I am a real professional.'

'What at?' I taunted.

'I could beat you any time on any course,' he boasted.

'Prove it.'

'You are rubbish. I wipe you out altogether.'

'Put your money where your mouth is.'

Fumio Ogino was not used to being insulted about his golfing prowess and it really hurt him. Signalling his men to release me, he stepped right up to glare wildly at me before crossing to my bedside telephone. He snatched up the receiver, dialled a number than had an aggressive exchange with someone at the other end of the line. Unable to follow a word, I gathered that he had won the argument when he put down the receiver and smiled in triumph.

'We go now, Alan Saxon.'

'Where?'

'To play golf.'

'At this time of night?'

'I prove who is best player.'

'Not a chance, mate.'

Fumio invented the rules with a stern countenance.

'You win, I respect,' he said.

'And if I lose?'

'They have you.'

He gestured to his brawny companions who laughed in unison. Their fun had only been postponed.

◇◇◇

The journey to the Wada International Country Club was the fastest and most bizarre I had ever made. Driven at top speed by Crew Cut One, the limousine blazed along the almost deserted express-way to carry me to my weird date with destiny. Fumio Ogino sat in the front seat with his back erect and his head held high, a master swordsman on his way to fight another duel, a champion prizefighter *en route* to another bloody victory in the ring. Consigned to the back seat alongside Crew Cut Two, I had time to meditate because my companion clearly spoke no English beyond a few words.

Twenty minutes looking at the back of Fumio's head were oddly productive. I learned some valuable information about him. Firstly, he did not in fact set the masseur on to me back at the hotel. He obviously lacked the imagination to devise such a trick. This was his world, sitting in a car with two gruesome thugs from Tokyo's underworld, planning my despatch on a golf course before enjoying my humiliation at the hands of his friends. Fumio did not want the managerial responsibilities of a Takeshi or the intensive work-load of a Yasayuki. He wanted to be a golfing playboy and his father's death had made that wonderfully possible.

He could also be absolved of any responsibility for the attempt on my life. Neither Crew Cut One nor his double would have much truck with cords and knives. Hard fists and brute strength were their stock-in-trade. Fumio had almost certainly unleashed them on Sam Limsong at some stage and then had the supreme pleasure of defeating the Thai golfer in a play-off. My execution was in reverse order. I would be pummelled by a superior golfer before being pounded by his horrendous playmates. It was a demoralising prospect.

We arrived at the golf course to find lights on in the club-house. Crew Cut Two had been appointed as my caddie and he yanked my golf bag out of the boot with the ease of a man lifting up a packet of toothpicks. As the four of us headed for the locker room, I realised how the contest would take place. There was a clanging sound from inside the clubhouse then bright light hit it from half a dozen different directions as giant floodlights came alive. The first three holes of the Wada International Country Club were illuminated for our benefit. Fumio's phone call at the hotel had summoned a reluctant club steward to open up especially for the occasion. One thing could be guaranteed. The floodlights would have been made by Ogino Electrical. I would be playing Fumio by the family version of the rising sun.

The odds were firmly stacked against me. Quite apart from the intimidatory presence of the two Crew Cuts, I was playing on a strange course against a man who knew it well. Fumio was on home ground. My only hope was to try to undermine some of his advantages. I fired the first few shots in the locker room.

'I spoke to Sam Limsong a few days ago,' I said.

'That man is scum!' hissed Fumio.

'He's a first-rate golfer.'

'I beat him last time we meet.'

'Only because your two pals here beat him first. Sam's got more feel for the game than you'll ever have. Nine times out of ten, he'll put you to shame.'

'Shut up about Limsong.'

'I believe that he knows Mitsu.'

'SHUT UP!'

He was shaking all over and waving a fist at me. That would take the edge off his first drive. There might be hope for me yet if I could somehow gain the initiative.

'We go,' announced Fumio. 'Three holes.'

'Best of three?'

'It will be me.'

'Don't count your chickens…'

We went out to the first hole for the midnight confrontation. I had never felt less like playing golf yet there had never been a time when I needed to be at the peak of my form. Percentage golf was out of the question. I had to take my courage in my hands and go for the flagstick. It was a case of win or weep.

The floodlights were truly impressive though I would have preferred to have seen them under other circumstances. A lofted drive might lift the ball up above the avenue of light but there would be no difficulty finding it once it hit the lush grass again. All three holes were bathed in artificial daylight and swept by a mild breeze. If nothing else, my ignominy would be extremely well-lit. Fumio took out a coin and won the toss. It gave him the honour.

The first hole was potentially the easiest, a 407-yards par-four with a sloping fairway that descended towards a reservoir. There were bunkers on the left to catch the hooked drive and several large trees which effectively blocked the line but it was not a hole to instil real fear on a normal day. This, however, was a very abnormal night and I found my mouth dry and my palms moist.

In a head-to-head clash of this nature, there was no margin for error. Fumio hit a flashy drive from the tee and skirted the trees to find a good position to the right of the fairway from which he could attack the green. He stood back to watch me.

Using my three-wood, I hit a powerful drive down the left-hand side that failed to fulfil its initial promise and found sand. My caddie sniggered but he was sharply reproved by Fumio. Rules and etiquette were to be strictly observed. Only if the impromptu game were taken seriously could it have any value. Fumio was a true golfer. He did not wish to beat me by any means other than superior ability. I was forced into other stratagems. As we strode down the slope together, I tried to ruffle his feathers.

'What was Yasayuki doing here today?'

'Yasayuki?'

'He's not interested in golf at all, is he?'

'You saw him here?'

'In the clubhouse. It was such a surprise after what he'd said to me at your party. About your career, I mean.'

'What did he say?'

'It wasn't very complimentary,' I lied. 'Maybe we should forget the whole thing.'

'What did Yasayuki say about me?' he demanded.

'Only that you'd never make it to the top. He said you didn't have the technique or stamina for tournament golf.'

'He knows nothing about it!'

'I'm only telling you what he said.'

'Yasayuki had no business being here!'

I stirred as merrily as I could and increased Fumio's ire but it did not help my own second shot. Playing out of sand with an awkward lie, the best I could manage was to get within forty yards of the green. Fumio made crisp work of his own second shot, aiming for the flag and rolling to within six feet of it. In rousing his anger, I seemed to have improved his accuracy. I got down in five. His birdie put him one hole ahead. Two more to play.

The second hole was a huge par-five that played every inch of its 595 yards. The tee shot involved a drive uphill to a narrow fairway with every encouragement for a sliced shot to hit the bank on the right and bounce back on to the fairway. The left side plunged down to an out-of-bounds fence so hooking had to be avoided at all costs. Fumio's drive scorned all hazards and finished up on the top of the hill. I almost matched him with my tee shot but when we reached our balls we could still not see the green. We had to hit our second shots down a corridor of pines. It was only with the third shot that the hole's true merit was revealed. Our target lay below us. It was a massive green curving along the side of a lake with a forested hill as a backdrop. A large bunker guarded the entrance. I played first and hit sand again but Fumio also came to grief. He seemed pleased with his shot at first but the distant plop into the water made him curse. It cost him the stroke that separated us. We were now level. One hole to play.

'Did you know about Packwood Heath?' I asked.

'What?'

'A course in England. Your father wanted to buy it. I wonder why he didn't consult you, Fumio. I mean, you're supposed to be the golfer, aren't you?'

'It was just a business investment.'

'Doki Securities are after it as well.'

'Who told you that?'

'Superintendent Ushiba. Didn't you know *that* either?'

But my attempt to unsettle him backfired. Instead of losing his concentration, he only stiffened his resolve to play the closing hole with a flourish. It was a 180-yards par-three of the kind that can give even the most battle-hardened veterans severe palpitations. The third hole called for a tee shot over glistening blue water to a small green with formidable bunkers all round it. Short but lethal, it was one of the most feared holes on the course and it required the utmost respect. Fumio gave it just that. His tee shot was unspectacular but safe, thudding into the turf some twenty yards or more from the cup. I mixed caution with adventure, hitting the ball higher and losing sight of it in the dark sky for a few seconds. When it finally landed, I gave a grunt of relief. I was fifteen feet from the cup.

Fumio excelled himself. After sizing up his putt, he hit it with what looked like perfect weight and line and my heart constricted. But it died some eighteen inches short of the target, leaving him a near-certain par. Only a brilliant putt could beat him. He would not settle for a halved hole. There had to be a winner and I was given a faint chance. I went into my usual routine and examined the shot from a variety of angles while Fumio—to his credit—watched in silence from the shadows. It was when I began to crouch off my ball that I got my injection of luck. Crew Cut One was holding the flagstick at the back of the green. I only glanced at him but that spilt-second was the difference between victory and defeat. The sight of the flagstick nudged my memory. I knew where I had seen the gold ring before. Excitement flooded through me and gave me a new confidence. My putt was firm and well-judged. It dropped into the hole with a decisive clunk.

Crew Cut Two immediately threw my bag to the ground and came menacingly across to me but Fumio's voice stopped him. Seething with annoyance at himself, my adversary nevertheless played to the rules. He offered me a curt handshake then reinforced it with a polite bow. Convinced that he would trounce me, he was abject in defeat but he accepted it with a degree of grace.

'We will drive you back to your hotel,' he said.

'Drop me off somewhere else, please.'

'Where?'

'At the film lab.'

'Why?'

'I have to see a man about a gold ring.'

◇◇◇

The return journey to Tokyo was a vast improvement on the outward trip. Fumio Ogino sat beside me in the rear of the limousine, now able to look back on his defeat with a sort of tattered dignity.

He freely conceded his jealousy of me and explained how it had been promoted by his father's adulation for Alan Saxon and by the further praise heaped upon me by Sam Limsong. Before I'd even arrived in Tokyo, Fumio had marked me out as an enemy. Now that he'd found an element of truth in the eulogies I'd attracted, he was able to come to terms with them. By the time the car reached the film laboratory, he was asking my advice about his playing career.

They dropped me off and drove away. I had difficulty convincing the security staff to let me in but they relented when they understood who I was. Chiyo Takumi had shown me how to operate the playback machine to watch the unedited film that had so far been shot. The efficient Keiko had numbered and dated each can so I knew which one to select. Alone in a darkened room at the rear of the building, I spooled on the film then set it into motion. The shock of seeing myself talking to camera amused me for a moment but I was not there to be entertained. Somewhere in that day's filming was a sequence that would explain everything and I felt a surge of exhilaration when I eventually came to it.

Alan Saxon was putting towards the hole on a green that sloped up and away from him. The flagstick had been lifted out and used as a directional aid, pointing down to a cup that was partly obscured from me. My shot was straight and true but that was not what arrested my gaze. I was watching the left hand that was holding the flagstick. On its little finger was a tiny gold ring that glinted in the sun. The diamond shape confirmed its identity. As the camera pulled back, I was able to get a full-length picture of the man who had turned my visit to Japan into one long ordeal.

It was Hideo Nakane. I pressed a button and froze the frame. The gold ring was a dazzle on the flagstick. In that single image, so much now became clear but I was given no time at all to marshal the evidence. A door clicked behind me and a fluorescent light was switched on. Hideo Nakane was not relying on a cord or a knife this time. He was pointing a small revolver at me.

'I'm sorry, Alan. You should have gone home.'

'Not until this mess has been cleared up.'

'I gave you enough warning. That Japanese massage would have sent anyone else racing for the next plane to England.'

'I took the plane to Bangkok,' I said. 'That's when I should have rumbled you. Pretending to get me to Narita then deliberately crashing your car so that I'd miss my flight. Having a lift from us next morning so that you could pump me about what I'd found out from Sam Limsong.'

'He was an animal!' sneered Hideo.

'Sam really loved Mitsu.'

'She was *mine!* I loved her properly. I earned her.'

'Then why did she turn you down?'

'It was Shohei's fault. He should have controlled his daughter. He should have made her marry me.' Rancour was contorting his face and making his hand tremble. 'Shohei refused to do as I told him. That's why he had to go. He told me I'd *never* have Mitsu.'

'Wise man.'

'We were meant for each other!'

'Then why did you revolt her so much?'

'It's not true!'

'That's how it came across to me,' I said. 'Shohei should never have let you anywhere near her. What did you have on him?'

He grinned. 'Plenty. I was his chief translator. I got to see the most sensitive material that came into Ogino Electrical. They trusted me. I had access to everything.'

'Including details of Packwood Heath,' I ventured. 'How much did Doki Securities pay you for that information?'

'It wasn't the money, Alan. It was the revenge. The look on Shohei's face when he thought he'd be pipped to the post by someone else. It served him right.'

'Because he kept his daughter away from you.'

'He went back on his promise.'

'A promise that was exacted by blackmail,' I reminded. 'You were just a humble translator with the company. Wealthy men like Shohei Ogino would never choose a Hideo Nakane as their son-in-law. It was out of the question.'

'Mitsu and I would've been happy together.'

'She deserves better.'

'She'll get me.'

'Don't bank on it, Hideo.'

'There's only one person stopping me, Alan,' he said as he moved slowly closer. 'That's you. Once you're out of the way, it'll be plain sailing. Mitsu will come round.'

'Not in a million years.'

'You know nothing about it.'

'She confided in me. The main reason she got involved with Sam was to keep you at arm's length. You were a threat. She needed another man.' I had put more tremble into him. 'That's why you could never forgive Sam Limsong, wasn't it? Because he had what you wanted. Because you had a fixation that he'd come back for her one day. I thought Shohei had planted that bugging device but it was you. My trip to Bangkok gave you the chance to eavesdrop on Sam because he was your hated rival. He and Mitsu actually...'

'Be quiet!' he shouted.

'She preferred him.'

'Be quiet!' He held the gun in two hands to control the trembling. 'You don't know what was really going on.'

And I did not wait to hear it. Surprise was my only hope. I moved as swiftly as I could. Throwing the film spool up into his face, I hurled myself at him and knocked him backwards on to the floor, grabbing his wrist to twist the gun upwards. We grappled fiercely. The first two bullets sank in the ceiling. The next one shattered the fluorescent tube and brought the security men running. We kicked and gouged and rolled and fought. Hideo Nakane was a strong young man and I had the greatest difficulty in holding him. The fourth bullet went over my shoulder and smashed the tiny screen on which I had been watching the film. Flagstick and ring vanished from sight in a snowstorm of glass particles.

The security men helped to overpower him and to wrest the gun away but not before it had fired its last bullet. Hideo Nakane shot himself through the skull then collapsed in a pool of his own blood. They kindly lifted him off me.

◇◇◇

When the video was completed, we were duly paid and thanked and seen off at the airport. Mitsu and Chiyo both came to give me a parting kiss while Clive Phelps was taking a fond farewell of Keiko. There was another well-wisher who was keen to have a final word with me. Superintendent Akio Ushiba was chuckling happily again.

'We'll make a policeman out of you yet,' he said.

'I doubt it.'

'Hideo was so plausible. He even injured himself to make it look as if he'd been threatened as well. He fooled me, Alan. I'm the first to admit it.'

'How long had he been blackmailing Shohei?'

'For years. But Yasayuki was another victim.'

'Yasayuki?'

'Yes,' explained Ushiba. 'Hideo stumbled on something down at the research lab in Yokohama. Designed and tested by Yasayuki himself for production abroad. In one of their English subsidiaries, actually.' The chuckle ripened. 'Just like the instructional video. An Anglo-Japanese venture.'

'What was the invention?'

'A new UHF radio.'

'How could Hideo blackmail him over that?'

'It was designed for battlefield use and sold to Iraq.'

'No more explanation was needed. Newspapers had kept me abreast of the enormous opposition to the proposal to deploy Japanese troops as part of the U.N. Force in the Middle East. If those troops were involved in a war in the gulf, they would be up against equipment designed and manufactured by Ogino Electrical. The company image would be seriously tarnished if that information ever became public.

'One consolation for you, anyway,' said Ushiba.

'We saved Packwood Heath.'

'Yes. You make a video in Tokyo and rescue a golf course in Northants. When we widened our investigations to include them, Doki Securities pulled out of the deal.'

'Nice to know we had some impact.'

'You had lots, Alan. That's why I'll re-read your book with fresh interest.' He produced my autobiography and handed it over with a pen. 'Can you sign it, please?'

I scribbled something inside the front cover and handed the book back to him. Akio Ushiba read the inscription.

'Earthquakes, thunderbolts, fires, fathers, policemen.'

He was still chuckling as we walked away.